BROMPTON MANOR

BROMPTON MANOR

•

Susan Ralph

AVALON BOOKS
NEW YORK

Fic

Published by Thomas Bouregy & Co., Inc.
160 Madison Avenue, New York, NY 10016

Library of Congress Cataloging-in-Publication Data

Ralph, Susan, 1938–
   Brompton Manor / Susan Ralph.
         p. cm.
   ISBN-13: 978-0-8034-9817-4 (alk. paper)
   ISBN-10: 0-8034-9817-9 (alk. paper)
   I. Title.

PS3608.A6954B76 2007
813'.6—dc22

                                        2006028588

PRINTED IN THE UNITED STATES OF AMERICA
ON ACID-FREE PAPER
BY HADDON CRAFTSMEN, BLOOMSBURG, PENNSYLVANIA

To my husband, daughters, grandchildren,
and sons-in-law who surround me with love.

Chapter One

"This is far's I go, ma'am. Brompton Manor's on the other side of them gates. 'Bout twenty minutes on foot up to the Manor house, I reckon."

Amilie Jasperton's fluttering heartbeat quieted as her eyes skimmed across the imposing building visible through the trees.

Sitting atop the apex of a hill, the sprawling structure reigned over undulating, green lawns that tumbled downward till they met the road. Rays of sunlight struck the exterior and splayed across the buff-colored stones to make the large house appear warm and welcoming.

Gathering the skirt of her dress in one hand, Amilie gripped the backboard of the dray with her free hand and hopped down. At the rear of the dray, she pulled her small scuffed, leather valise off and set it in the road, then holding her breath, tugged at her larger valise until

1

it teetered on the edge of the dray's flat bed. Clutching the carrying straps of the valise in both hands she pulled the heavy bag free and set it beside the smaller bag.

The driver of the rig clucked his nag into motion and tipped his hat. "Take care, miss."

Amilie waited until he drove off, then dragged her valises to the scrolled, wrought-iron gate, got them around to the other side and settled them behind one of the stone pillars that anchored either side of the gate.

Sighing, she tipped over the larger valise, plopped down on the top, stretched out her legs and reached into her reticule in search of her handkerchief.

The side of her hand brushed against the invitation that brought her to this unfamiliar place. She pulled it out and placed it in her lap. Her heartbeat drummed in her ears.

Everything she knew and loved belonged to someone else now. The vicarage, in need of paint; the worn upholstered chair in which she tucked herself to read; the bed where her dreams enlivened her nights; the church with the pianoforte where she practiced her music and the needs and joys of her father's parish were no longer available to her.

A new vicar presided in her father's place, his wife fulfilled her mother's duties, his children bedded down in her attic room.

An orphanage was the only home her father knew before he was grown. The structure she could see through the trees was the home of her mother before her mother was banished from her family. Amilie was never told why. She knew her mother's parents were the earl and countess of Brompton and little else.

Six months ago a fire at an inn where her parents had taken accommodation for the night took their lives. She had been left with meager resources and bereft of family.

The local squire offered her a place in his household as assistant to the governess. She accepted the position, grateful for his kindness and for his protection.

And then, five days ago, the post brought an invitation from the countess of Brompton. The grandparents she never met and knew almost nothing about were inviting her to visit them at Brompton Manor.

After recovering from the shock of learning her mother's estranged parents knew of her existence and where to find her, she sought the squire's advice. At his urging, and with the promise she could return to his household at any time, she had posted her acceptance and bought a coach ticket.

Amilie's fingers found the handkerchief she was searching for. She took it from her reticule, wiped the moisture from her forehead and patted the cloth over her cheeks and chin.

This morning, when she arrived at the inn in her home village from which the post and stage coaches arrived and departed, the area was already bustling with activity. Horses were being hitched, coaches were being loaded with all manner of bags and pouches and trunks, passengers milled about, searching for their coach or purchasing a ticket at the last minute.

When she stepped up into the coach for which she

held a ticket, she learned every seat inside would be taken. For the entire eight hours it took to get to the coach stop nearest Brompton Manor, a coaching inn located within a mile of the gates of Brompton Manor, she had been squashed between two, well-fed female passengers who chattered the entire time.

By the time she stepped down from the coach for the last time, her dress was wrinkled, her stomach was unsettled, and her spirit was depressed.

She hired the dray to transport her the remaining distance to Brompton Manor's gate and handed a stable boy a coin to load her valises on the dray's bed. The fresh air, the silent driver, and the room to move her arms about freely had lifted her spirit some, but with each turn of the dray's wheel more of her will to go through with her visit slipped away.

She fingered the invitation. If she turned back now, she would spend the rest of her life without the answers she was seeking. Her mother's early life and the reason for her banishment would forever be a mystery.

Adjusting her thin cloak about her shoulders, Amilie pulled herself out of her reverie, looked around and let the beauty and quiet surroundings ease her anxiety. Leaving her heavy valises by the pillar, she stepped onto the carriage lane and started walking toward the Manor house.

Within minutes, her stomach began to grumble, protesting the grease-laden stew she had eaten at one of the coach stops along the route. Swallowing hard, she prayed for the contents of her stomach to stay down, clapped a hand across her mouth, closed her eyes and stood still until her stomach quieted. Then, with gritted teeth and tightened lips, she continued on.

Three-fourths of the way to the Manor house from the main road, the packed dirt of the carriage lane abutted the wooden planks of a bridge that arched over a stream that widened into a lake on the opposite side.

She stopped at the highest point of the arch, leaned her elbows atop the railing, cupped her face in her hands and let the quiet of the scene envelop her. Trills of conversation between the birds refreshed her ears. Sweet scents carried by the light breeze removed the coach odor of sweat and dirt and moldering hay from her memory.

She scanned the circumference of the lake. In the distance, a pair of white swans slipped into the water. She wanted to stay in this idyllic place, in this undemanding time, forever. But she could not stop. Not now. Not when she was so close to learning the answers to her questions.

Reaching up, she tightened the ribbons of her bonnet and set one foot down in front of the other until she stood in front of a pair of massive, carved wood doors.

She grasped the bottom edge of the shiny, gold, doorknocker, lifted the clapper high and banged it against the strike plate.

The door edged back exposing a liveried footman with a ramrod back and a sour expression on his face. His eyes glared at her. "Servants' entrance 'round back."

With no calling card to hand him, she lifted her chin and shoulders and announced herself. "Miss Amilie

Jasperton, the earl of Brompton's granddaughter. I am expected," she said, returning the footman's fierce glare.

The footman kept his haughty countenance, but swung the door wide and moved aside.

With a step across the stone threshold, Amilie found herself in an oval reception hall four times the size of the parlor in the vicarage. The furnishings were of a quality she imagined afforded only to members of the ruling class. She tried not to gape as her eyes explored the cavernous space.

A diamond pattern of polished black and white marble squares sparkled on the floor; two niches in a far wall displayed matched porcelain vases that looked as tall as she, and a white marble staircase was centered by a spill of red carpet that ran down the steps.

Amilie twined her fingers together, tilted her head to one side and returned her eyes to the footman.

"Wait here, miss," he said, wrinkling his nose and pointing to a chair.

His receding steps echoed through the reception hall. Amilie remained standing as her anxieties gathered into a steamed pudding lump in the pit of her stomach.

Her knees trembled; her eyes became watery. She clamped her lips tight and lifted her chin—determined not to give way to her queasy stomach, wobbly knees, and teary eyes.

The sound of door hinges squeaking interrupted her faltering resolve to remain in this alien place. Hoping to hide her fears and quiet her trembling hands, she straightened her shoulders and fixed the corners of her lips into a smile.

A dour-faced woman, wearing a plain mobcap and a dress fashioned from cheap muslin, emerged from around the back of the staircase. A ring of keys dangled from a chatelaine hanging at her waist. Trailing behind her was a young maid dressed in a similar manner.

"I am Mrs. Burton, Brompton Manor's house-keeper," the older woman said. She stood in front of Amilie, blocking her from stepping farther inside the entrance hall. "Your arrival was not expected today."

All of the bravado she had summoned when confronting the footman was gone. Eight months beyond her seventeenth year and this austere woman with her haughty manner made her feel like a child. Her stomach rumbled; the greasy stew threatened again. She bit her bottom lip and inhaled a shuddering breath.

"Her ladyship's traveling carriage departed from here early this morning to fetch you. It was to deliver you here tomorrow," Mrs. Burton said.

"My apologies for causing an inconvenience." Amilie heard the tremble in her voice. "Notice of a carriage being sent for me failed to arrive before I set out." Amilie pulled the sides of her cloak tight across her body, and took a step toward the door. "Until tomorrow, then."

The housekeeper's keys jangled as she turned and stepped aside. "You are here, miss. I will make accommodation."

Amilie felt the chill in the housekeeper's grudging offer. She had no idea how to react to the servants in this fine house. She forced her lips into a bigger smile.

The housekeeper gestured for the young woman standing behind her to step forward. "Helaine will show you to your apartments, miss."

The young maid stepped around the housekeeper and curtsied. The sparkle in her eyes belied a sober countenance and presented Amilie her first comfort since the door of Brompton Manor opened.

"My valises sit by the gatepost. If a handcart is available . . ."

The housekeeper sniffed a rebuke. "A footman will be sent for your valises, Miss Jasperton. Helaine is available for any other needs you may have."

Helaine curtsied again and started toward the marble staircase. Amilie followed Helaine up the marble steps and then up a staircase of polished, dark wood.

Helaine turned right on the landing and hurried down a corridor lined with closed doors and around a corner and down another corridor. Weary from her travel and awed by the size and elegance of the interior of Brompton Manor, Amilie labored to keep up.

Finally, Helaine halted before a door and pushed down the handle. "Your apartments, miss."

Amilie looked through the open doorway into an intimate sitting room. Her audible gasp sounded loud in her ears; her hand flew upward to cover her mouth.

A sitting room.

She stepped inside. Her eyes circled the room taking

everything in. Pale, rose-color fabric covered two wing chairs drawn close to the fire grate. Curtains were fashioned from the same fabric and the walls were covered in a deeper rose color silk. The accent color of clotted cream scribed a stripe through the wall covering, fashioned a swirl of pattern in the upholstery fabric and peeked from the string fringe of the tasseled trim on the curtains.

Helaine pointed to a door in the left wall. "Your bedchamber, miss."

Amilie peeked around the doorframe of the second room. The bedchamber was larger than the sitting room. A pair of tall windows matched the two windows in the sitting room. A four-poster bed was hung with silk drapes fashioned of the same fabric used in the sitting room.

Entering the bedchamber, she sat down on the edge of the bed, ran her hands along the smooth fabric of the counterpane and fought a desire to lie down. She pushed herself to her feet and walked back into the sitting room.

Helaine was kneeling in front of the fire grate adding coals and humming under her breath.

"This is all so grand, Helaine. Finer then anything I have known," Amilie said as she stood next to the chimneypiece, watching as Helaine poked at the coals.

Helaine got to her feet. Her lips retained a neutral line, her eyes showed no emotion, except for a brief glimmer of understanding that flashed through them. "Yes, miss. Your supper and your valises are on their way."

After Helaine left, Amilie drifted between the two rooms mindlessly opening the doors and drawers of the case furniture. On her second go around, she moved to stand at one of the sitting room windows. From these front-facing windows, she could see into the cobbled entrance courtyard and down the front lawns. A flicker of motion through the trees lining the carriage lane caught her eye. She watched as a pony cart moved up the lane toward the Manor house. When it came into the courtyard area, she saw her valises were aboard before the cart rounded the corner of the house and disappeared.

Chill air penetrated the window glass. She shivered and moved away to sit by the fire. The apprehension she felt over meeting her mother's parents and the overwhelming beauty of the grounds and the house had damped her awareness of her exhaustion. But now, in the quiet of this intimate, cozy room fatigue lowered her eyelids.

She placed her cheek against the wing of the chair and drifted into sleep.

The jiggle of the door handle of her sitting room woke her. The door hinges creaked. Alarm roiled her senses. She raised her eyelids enough to see the footman standing in her open door, holding her valises.

"Miss?" inquired a whispery voice.

Amilie lifted her head and scrubbed at her eyes with her fists. "Come in," she instructed, her voice thick with sleep.

Bearing a silver tray, Helaine followed the footman

into the room. Visible atop the tray were a teapot and several serving dishes embellished with a blue, floral pattern rimmed with gold. The footman vanished through the door of the bedchamber. Helaine began arranging the items on the tray around the circular top of a table that stood between the windows.

"While you enjoy your supper, I will unpack your valises and put your things away, miss."

Amilie nodded. Her attention focused on the items sitting on the table. Three different meat offerings and a place setting of translucent china and silver utensils seemed overly lavish for a weekday supper. She sat motionless for several seconds before picking up the soupspoon and dipping it into the pale green soup.

As her stomach warmed from the turtle soup, her eyes filled with unbidden tears that overflowed and trickled down her cheeks. She rose from the table, returned to her chair by the fire and turned toward the grate to hide her face from view as she brushed at the tears with her fingers.

Everything about this place was strange to her. No one in her father's parish lived in such a grand style as this, not even the squire, the most prosperous land owner in the county.

She barely knew Helaine, and with the exception of the housekeeper and the footman, she had not spoken with anyone. She did not know whom to trust with her loneliness, or with whom she could share her fear about fitting into this new world. She did not know who would understand her concern over being declared unworthy and banished from this house like her mother.

"Miss?" Helaine asked breaking into her thoughts. "Are you ready to prepare for bed?"

Amilie got to her feet. "Lay out my nightrail, Helaine, and then you may go."

"Where should I put your books, miss?"

"Leave them on the table between the windows. I may sit by the fire and read for a time."

Helaine gathered the supper dishes and stacked them atop the tray. "Do you prefer coffee or chocolate in the morning, miss?"

Chocolate? She did not know what chocolate was. Was it similar to tea?

Amilie turned and looked at Helaine. "Chocolate," she declared, punctuating her choice with a quick nod of her head.

"Her ladyship expects your appearance at ten o'clock tomorrow morning."

Amilie swallowed hard. In the morning she would meet her mother's mother. A woman who was capable of banishing her only child and never yielding. What could such a woman be like?

Amilie moved to the table where her books were piled one atop the other. She picked up the top book from the short stack. Her books, her clothing, her mother's gold locket, the small, inlaid box her mother stored her few keepsakes in, and a partially finished canvas were the only things she could claim as hers. Holding the book in both hands, she pressed it to her mid-section, right beneath her heart, and kept her back to the door until she heard the click of the latch.

"Marlton."

Amilie was jolted from a deep sleep when the shout from the courtyard penetrated through her bedchamber windows.

She bolted upright, clutching the bedcovers. Where was she? Panic grabbed her heart. And then she re-membered.

"Marlton, my horse," the same booming voice shat-tered the early morning quiet a second time.

Amilie touched her toes to the floor and swept her bedcovers aside. Crossing to a window, she peered out in hopes of spotting the culprit who felt free to make a loud commotion so early in the day.

A lone gentleman sat astride a sleek, long-legged, chestnut horse in the entrance courtyard. Leaning for-ward in the saddle and cupping a gloved hand around his mouth, he was prepared to bugle another summons.

Before he did, a lad dashed from around the corner of the house into the courtyard, approached the horse and rider, nodded to the gentleman and took the horse's reins from him. The rider lowered his gloved hand but spoke in the same loud voice.

"Where is Marlton, Tom?"

"Gone to check one of the mares, sir."

"Rub down my horse and see he has water and feed. He has come a long distance."

"Yes, sir. Right away, Mr. Fitzhugh."

"You're a good lad, Tom. Grown some since I last saw you."

"Yes, sir. Right out of me clothes, sir."

The rider threw back his head and indulged himself in a full-throated laugh, then, with an athlete's grace, he dismounted and with long, quick strides started toward the entrance steps.

Amilie stared at the man's long legs and his muscled thighs encased in a pair of tight riding breeches. Whoever this inconsiderate gentleman was, his body matched the prized configuration of a racehorse and his pace matched the speed of the horses she watched as they competed in the local races.

If she was fortunate, she would not have occasion to encounter this rude man during her stay here. His face was clean-shaven, he was well-dressed, but his manner was overbearing . . . her father would have said bumptious.

Chapter Two

Amilie snuggled back under her bedcovers, too alert now for sleep. Lying on her side, she curled her knees to her chest and let her imagination drift until the squeak of her bedchamber door heralded the start of the next act in this strange drama.

"Miss. Time to be up and about."

Amilie rolled over and watched as Helaine poured a brownish liquid into a china cup, then set the cup down on the nightstand. "Your chocolate, miss. I will see to the coals and keep the wash water warm while you have your morning cup."

Amilie stayed beneath the covers until Helaine moved out of the bedchamber. Then, sitting up, she picked up the cup. The steam from the hot liquid carried an unfamiliar perfume to her nose. She dipped the tip of her tongue into the liquid. The taste of chocolate was both sweet and bitter. It tasted nothing like tea or coffee. Chocolate was delicious. She would order chocolate every morning. And she would not rise from bed until she drank it all.

"You should dress and eat some breakfast, miss," Helaine said from the doorway. "We best set off for her ladyship's apartments soon."

Amilie accepted Helaine's assistance with her toilette then nibbled at a piece of toast, swallowed two bites of coddled egg, and declared herself ready.

She followed Helaine as the maid scurried through a maze of corridors and down a staircase then paused to open a door and motioned for Amilie to enter. "Wait here, miss," she said, closing the door. Amilie was alone in an elegantly appointed room. All four walls were covered with portraits and landscapes in carved, gilt frames.

Fidgeting with nervous energy, Amilie smoothed back her hair, adjusted the neckline of her dress, and rubbed her hands down the sides of her skirt. She would ask directly the questions she wanted answers to. Once she had her answers, she would be free to leave here at any time.

She braced herself, steadying her nerves. Today's events had provided her with another question, perhaps more pressing at the moment. Who was the unmannered gentleman shouting his demands in the courtyard this morning?

The sound of a door opening caused her to look up. A woman, around her mother's age, stood in the doorway to an adjoining room. "The countess of Brompton," she announced in clear, rounded tones and stepped aside.

A tall, thin woman, with hair the color of rain clouds piled into a pouf atop her head, glided into the room. A pair of ice-blue eyes scoured Amilie.

"Turn, child," the countess of Brompton commanded.

Amilie began to do as told, but the room spun in front of her eyes like a toy whirligig in a strong wind. A solid black screen descended in front of her eyes.

"Miss Jasperton? Miss Jasperton?"

Amilie opened her eyes and blinked at the brightness of the light. The concerned face of the woman who had announced Lady Brompton hovered over her. She felt the coolness of a damp cloth pressed against her brow.

"I am so sorry . . ." she began.

"Sit up, dear. If you are able," commanded the unmistakable voice of the countess of Brompton.

Amilie used her elbows to raise her back off the floor, then struggled to her feet and dipped a curtsy. "My profound apologies, Lady Brompton. I. . . ."

"You are the image of your mother."

"Thank you." The mention of her mother startled her. She must remain guarded in her conversation until she learned the reason she had been invited here.

"Be seated, Amilie, and inform me about your education and your training."

Amilie sat on the edge of the chair seat, folded her hands in her lap, and forced her lips into a smile. "My parents schooled me at home. I read, write, and cipher.

I read Latin and Greek. Mother taught me to read and speak French. I am versed in the Bible.

"I am pleased. And what of your training?"

"I am skilled with a needle. I play the pianoforte and sing."

"And ride?"

"No."

"And you have been given lessons in dance and deportment?"

"Father thought my deportment well attended by my mother. Lessons in dance were arranged, but circumstances intervened."

"Your father's assessment of your mother's ability to instruct you properly was correct, of course, and it was wise of him to see to your education." The countess of Brompton dropped her voice to a mere whisper, but kept her eyes focused on Amilie. "Were you raised in a cheerful home?"

Amilie noted a sad wistfulness in the countess of Brompton's voice. "My father's sprightly, good humor filled our home with laughter and merriment. But his responsibilities as vicar were of the highest and most sobering concern to him."

Lady Brompton bowed her head and did not move for a time. When she raised her head, a smile softened her features, her eyes glistened and she changed the direction of their talk. "I shall engage a dancing master for you, one who instructs not only in dance, but in posture, grace, and the etiquette of the ballroom. Our groom will provide you riding lessons."

Amilie's caution dissolved like ice in a tropical sun. All of her reserve was replaced by her excitement over the news she was to have riding lessons. "An opportunity to learn to ride is an unexpected delight, and I will appreciate the instruction of a dance master. I looked forward to joining in our local assemblies before. . . ." Amilie's voice faltered, she bowed her head and sniffed, but managed to restrain her tears.

The countess of Brompton nodded and rose to her feet. "I am pleased by you, Amilie." Then she vanished into the adjoining room and the door shut behind her.

Amilie sprang to her feet and curtsied. She was alone with no idea how to proceed. Fear nibbled at her meager breakfast. Without someone to lead her back to her apartments, she would never find her way.

The clock on the fireplace mantle ticked off the minutes as she lingered in the room waiting for someone to come to her rescue. When the passing of time shortened the day by twenty minutes, she decided her only recourse was to venture into the hall in search of help.

She grasped the knob of the door through which she had entered the room at the exact moment the opposite door opened and the woman assisting Lady Brompton stepped back into the room.

"Helaine has been summoned."

Amilie experienced such sudden relief from her building tension that her knees buckled and forced her back into the chair. "I shall wait here, then," she said to the woman's departing back.

* * *

Safely back in her apartments, Amilie broached the idea to Helaine of touring the gardens visible through the windows along one of the corridors they had traipsed down.

"A splendid idea, miss. The gardens at Brompton Manor are lovely. We could inspect those closest to the house after your lunch, if you wish.

"Then we shall stroll about out-of-doors this afternoon."

"Yes, miss." Helaine made a deep curtsy. "I will bring your lunch, miss."

"Only tea, Helaine.

"If I may be bold, miss."

"Of course. Say what you wish."

"You should try to eat something, miss. You have not eaten much since you arrived here."

"Some soup along with the tea then."

"Yes, miss. And Cook made fresh biscuits this morning."

"And include one of Cook's biscuits."

Amilie located her needlework canvas and sat down to work the small, unfinished section. Sorting through her thoughts as she sorted through the silk threads, she snipped a length of a bright, pink thread and pushed the cut end through the eye of a needle.

Concentrating on her stitches, she blocked all unwanted thoughts from disturbing her, and with each push of her needle through the mesh, she gained a sense of accomplishment. The shape of a bright, pink flower emerged and her vigorous effort rewarded her with a finished canvas by the time Helanie returned with the lunch tray. Helaine set the tray down, arranged the contents on the table, and went into Amilie's bedchamber.

Amilie drank the tea and finished the soup, then ate a few bites of the ham and all of the cold jelly that had been included.

When Helaine came back into the sitting room Amilie presented her with a grin. "I am happy you thought to include extras on my lunch tray, Helaine," she said picking up the ginger biscuit and taking a bite. "Both my spirits and my appetite increased as I worked my canvas."

Helaine removed the soiled lunch dishes from the table and placed them back on the tray.

"Have you your bonnet?" Amilie asked.

"Yes, miss. 'Tis on a table in the hall."

"Then leave the tray, and we shall be off."

"This sunshine is a joyous blessing," Amilie said as they strolled down a path toward a brick-walled garden. "At home rain fell every day for a month before I left. The damp caused mold to grow everywhere and the abundance of water turned the dirt roads and lanes into mud. It is a welcome treat, finding myself outside without water dripping from my bonnet and pattens strapped to my shoes."

"We are fortunate here, miss. We have long periods when the sun shines. Everyone is happy when we leave the lowering skies and fog of London and return to the country."

"How many go to London?"

"A few always go with his lordship when he goes. Most of us go during the Season."

The Season. Amilie only knew what a Season involved from what she read in books. If she stayed at Brompton Manor, would they expect her to go to London for the Season too? The prospect of doing so threatened to spoil her enjoyment of the tour of the nearby gardens.

They went through a brick archway that gave entry to the walled garden. At the far end, pacing back and forth between the two sidewalls, his hands clasped behind his back, his head lowered, his stride subdued, was the gentleman Amilie had seen shouting in the courtyard.

"Perhaps you wish an unoccupied garden, miss." Helaine said.

Before Amilie could decide her preference, the gentleman raised his head and glanced in their direction. "Hello," he called in a thunderous voice.

Amilie eyed the gentleman hastening toward them. His strong legs allowed him to close the distance between their positions in seconds—far faster than Amilie could order her thinking. The broad smile plastered on his face and the lack of tension in his countenance, reassured her he carried no anger over being disturbed.

"Allow me," he said and bowed. "Colin Fitzhugh, late of America.

Amilie stood mute—staring into his sea blue eyes flecked through with green—awed by the vibrant energy that radiated from him and the sense of command he exuded.

"And you are Miss Jasperton, I presume?" he continued with amusement enlivening his eyes.

Amilie found her voice. "Your presuming is correct, Mr. Fitzhugh." She tilted her head and studied his face for a moment. His expression was only encouraging. "Miss Amilie Jasperton, late of the village of Chesterwold."

"May I express the pleasure I enjoyed when learning of your presence at Brompton Manor, Miss Jasperton. Rather boring in the country when no guests are here. For what number of days are you planning to stay?"

"I do not know, sir."

"I will be here until the end of the month. I look forward to seeing you again, Miss Jasperton. Now I shall adjourn and let you enjoy the delights of this fine garden."

After executing a deep bow, Colin Fitzhugh disappeared before Amilie could catch her breath.

Sinking down on a bench beside one of the planting beds, she examined their encounter. Had Mr. Fitzhugh winked at Helaine as he moved by her?

"Sit down and tell me about Mr. Fitzhugh, Helaine. His shouting in the courtyard this morning startled me out of my sleep so suddenly it took me several moments before I could recall where I was."

"What words did he shout, miss?"

"Marlton. And then, Marlton, my horse."

Helaine laughed a gay, rippling laugh. "Marlton is

one of the undergrooms, miss. But Mr. Fitzhugh's shouting was to alert everyone of his return. The servants at Brompton Manor spoil him worse than his lordship does, and I do believe, Mr. Fitzhugh's sense of himself is swelled." Helaine sounded a giggle and pressed a finger against her lips.

"And what is this gentleman's relationship to the earl and countess of Brompton?"

"Mr. Fitzhugh is his lordship's ward, taken in at a young age and given the upbringing of an heir, which he can never be. The Brompton title and estates pass to a distant cousin."

"But in the meantime, Mr. Fitzhugh acts as though he is the heir?"

"I think not, miss. But he has a grand zest for life and a real fondness for the only home he knows. We grew up together here, me mum was Cook."

"She is retired?"

"In a way. She passed. Three years ago next month."

"I am sorry, Helaine. It is painful to lose a parent. I lost both of mine. Six months ago."

"Yes, miss. I see the sorrow worrying your eyes."

"Sometimes, when I do not expect it, a deep sadness settles on me."

"It takes time, miss, but the pain does ease some."

Amilie looked directly at Helaine. "Do you know the reason my mother was banished?"

"It is not my place to talk about such things, miss."

"No. I suppose not." Amilie looked down at the

ground and ran the toe of her half-boot through the spiky grass. Helaine touched her arm.

"Her ladyship is kind. Wait for her to explain, in her own way, when she is ready."

Amilie unfolded her arms and legs, stood and breathed in a large quantity of the scented, garden air. "We are damping the beauty of the garden, spreading our gloom about. A closer inspection of those colorful blooms in the bed by the far wall should cheer us."

Standing by the bed of luminous, yellow flowers, they filled their eyes with the cheering sight. A musty odor sailed upward from the rich loam of the bed to add its earthy scent to the pleasure of the moment.

They started back to the opening in the garden wall in a companionable silence. Emerging through the arched opening to the lawns, Amilie spotted a large building to her left. "What is that odd-looking building? "There . . . ," she said pointing ". . . the one with the tall windows?"

" 'Tis the orangery, miss. Come, see inside."

The air inside the orangery was warm and moist and fragrant. Trees, their roots embedded in big terra-cotta pots sitting on the flagstone floor, were green and full. A wooden bench nestled against one wall, its plank top covered by smaller pots filled with an assortment of plants.

"What are those plants with the orange-gold flowers?"

"Calendula, miss. The Calendula flowers have many

uses. Some people say they are a comforter of hearts and spirits. I am not sure of the truth of that, but the dried blossoms mixed with oil and melted beeswax makes a fine ointment for scrapes and such."

Amilie bent her head, sniffing the strong scent of the Calendula. "I would like to learn about all of the plants growing here and the uses they can be put to."

"I could teach you some, miss."

"I would like that."

"Many of these plants come from far away, miss. Look there, above your head."

Amilie followed the direction of Helaine's finger. Big, orange globes hung from the branches of several of the nearby trees.

"Oranges, miss."

"May we take one?"

A loud harrumph sounded. Amilie's heart jumped.

"Why did you bring a thief in here to steal my fruit, Helaine?"

" 'Tis hardly a thief. 'Tis his lordship's granddaughter."

A short, muscular man, wearing a frayed cap and pulling work gloves from his hands, came around the corner and ambled down the aisle. "A pleasure, miss," he said giving Amilie a deferential nod. "You wish one of my prized oranges?"

"I have never seen an orange tree laden with fruit before, and I have tasted an orange only once. My sincere apology."

"You promise not to tell Cook," he said as he

plucked a fat orange ball from one of the trees. "A rat helped himself, without permission, I'll tell her when she comes to count her oranges."

Helaine snickered. "When his lordship began building the orangery, me mum would come every day, around sunset, to check on the progress. She was filled with pride to think she could have fresh fruit on her table year 'round."

The gardener offered the orange to Amilie. "When the exterior was finished, she came here every day to worry me about my plants. Now be off and enjoy the orange before you return to the Manor house and Cook catches you with it. Neither one of you resembles a rat."

The sound of giggles bounced off the glass panes as Amilie and Helaine headed for the door.

Halfway between the orangery and the Manor house, the two young women sat down on a bench fitted beneath an arbor. Helaine removed the thin peel from the orange and handed the fruit to Amilie who broke the orange into two pieces, and handed one of the halves to Helaine.

Laughing, Amilie licked the sweet juice of the orange from her fingers, pulled off a section and popped the piece of fruit into her mouth.

Once the delectable fruit had been enjoyed, Helaine stood up and dipped a deep curtsy to Amilie. "If I may be bold, miss," she said then paused a moment before she continued on in a rush of words. "It is concerning our relationship, miss." Helaine dropped her eyes. "I am in service here, and you are the granddaughter of the earl, miss. I overstepped my place today."

"But, Helaine, I don't think of myself as the granddaughter of an earl and have no idea how the granddaughter of an earl goes on."

"Here you are recognized as such. It is your place. And where there are servants and masters, it is important for everyone to keep to their place. Even below stairs, there is an order of rank."

"I will try to act accordingly from now on, but I am glad for today. You have made my time here easier, Helaine."

"I believe, miss, if you give your approval, I am to serve you as lady's maid."

Amilie looked at her feet, staring at the toes of her half boots. Her voice sounded flat as she responded to Helaine's statement. "Your service as lady's maid to me is approved."

Amilie rose, stared straight ahead, and started to walk toward the Manor house. Helaine followed a proper step behind.

Chapter Three

Helaine held up Amilie's one silk dress. "To wear at dinner, miss."

Amilie caressed the silky fabric. "After Papa said I was to attend the local assemblies, Mama fashioned this dress for me from one of her old gowns."

"A lovely dress, miss. His lordship is expected at table tonight."

Helaine picked up the ivory-backed hairbrush from the dressing table. She drew the bristles through Amilie's thick, wavy hair then fashioned the hair into a tumble of curls and pinned them to the top of Amilie's head. She freed several tendrils to curl a magical tease around Amilie's face and neck.

Amilie stared at the image of herself in the looking-glass. "You have done a wonderful job fashioning my hair, Helaine."

"Thank you, miss."

Amilie opened a drawer in the dressing table and took out her mother's gold locket. She held the locket in the center of her chest with the tip of one finger as Helaine fastened the clasp of the chain.

"There, miss. The clasp is closed."

Amilie removed her finger. Glints of candlelight sparked off the locket as it dropped into the valley between her breasts.

Slipping into her dress, Amilie moved her hands slowly down the silk fabric of the skirt then straightened her shoulders. "Are other people expected at table tonight?"

"Only her ladyship and Mr. Fitzhugh."

"At least there will be no strangers requiring me to carry on gay conversation. My spirit still pains me, despite my having breathed in the scent of the Calendula flowers."

Amilie moved a tendril of hair that had fallen across her eye. "Is the earl of Brompton a nice gentleman?"

"His lordship treats his servants well. His illness causes him a short temper some days, but in recent days his lordship is often his jolly self."

"Papa teased me often for my propensity to prattle. I shall try to curb my tongue so I do not annoy."

Helaine laughed. "A trait you inherited from his lordship, if I may be bold, miss."

After a long examination of her reflection in the looking glass, Amilie pronounced herself ready.

Helaine led the way down the stairs and through several new twists and turns of the Manor house.

"I despair of learning my way around this house, Helaine. Perhaps I should start out tomorrow and not worry about becoming lost. I shall count on you to organize a search party if you find me missing from my apartments."

"Of course, miss, but I am near finished with a map of each floor. Even after all my years here, I have to stop sometimes to think where I have got to."

Helaine left Amilie at the door of the drawing room where the family and guests gathered before dinner, the on-duty, liveried footman grasped gold door handles and swung open the carved, double doors. Amilie gasped. The grandeur of the drawing room, a room larger than the entire first floor of the vicarage, left her awestruck. Mirrors captured and reflected the candlelight from the burning candles protruding from numerous wall sconces and from three chandeliers hanging from the ceiling. The odor of cheap, tallow candles was not detected. Amilie was aghast at the extravagance of burning hundreds of prized beeswax candles when only the immediate family was present.

Near the fire, three people sat together in a grouping of chairs. The gray-haired Lady Brompton, the wavy, dark-haired Mr. Fitzhugh, and the bald pate with a fringe of wispy, gray hair circling between a set of elongated ears, must be the earl of Brompton.

The footman at the door drew himself up to announce her to the room.

Lady Brompton and Mr. Fitzhugh craned their necks in her direction and rose to their feet. Lady Brompton came toward her, meeting her halfway across the room.

"Amilie, you look lovely this evening." She took Amilie's elbow in her cupped hand and escorted her the remaining distance to the sitting area.

Amilie was grateful for the assistance. It was certain her feet were still attached, but she could no longer feel them.

Mr. Fitzhugh, wearing a jacket as dark as his hair, nodded his head and bowed to her; his misty, sea blue eyes examined her face and moved down to her slippers.

Lady Brompton leaned over and spoke directly into the ear of the baldheaded gentleman.

"Brompton, your granddaughter."

The earl of Brompton cleared his throat and looked up. His eyes were watery. He held a handkerchief to his nose and blew.

Amilie dipped a curtsy. "Your Lordship."

The earl squinted his eyes and cocked his head to one side as he studied her.

Amilie did not move until he turned away.

He wiped his eyes with fingers bent with age. "Lovely child. Resembles her mother," he said, his voice cracking.

Lady Brompton made a small motion to the footman at the door.

"Dinner is served." The stentorian voice of a pigeon-breasted man standing in the doorway to the drawing room rolled through the cavernous room.

The earl of Brompton's nod brought a footman who hovered close by to his side. Grasping the footman's extended hand the earl of Brompton planted his walking stick in the rug and pulled himself out of the chair.

Amilie took Fitzhugh's proffered arm, placing her hand atop his extended forearm, but directed her gaze away from this gentleman whose dancing eyes quickened her senses in a manner she had not experienced before.

Lady Brompton accepted Fitzhugh's other arm. With the footman's aid, the earl of Brompton began creeping forward. The others fell in behind. And in a slow procession, the party proceeded down the hall to the dining room.

Seated at the table across from Fitzhugh, Amilie kept her eyes trained on her place setting. The table accessories alone were intimidating—the tabletop was barely visible beneath various sized serving bowls and platters of food, and each place setting was laid with fine china, engraved silver utensils, and etched stemware. Candelabra lined the center of the table, their holders filled with more beeswax candles. Amilie thought she must look like a dull gray mouse in this room as brilliant as a peacock in full display.

She kept her focus on the items directly in front of her and served herself from the dishes within reach.

The earl dominated the conversation, launching into a story that repeated conversations and related amusing incidents from his yearly shooting parties.

Both Lady Brompton and Fitzhugh inserted an occasional anecdote when he paused to fork food into his mouth—anecdotes that often caused him great merriment.

Knowing none of the stories and none of the participants, Amilie only half-listened. Her papa would chuckle to see her tongue silenced, but would he approve her being here? Would her mother approve if she knew Amilie was visiting Brompton Manor? Amilie swallowed a bite of ham along with the lump in her throat.

The ordeal of her first formal dinner at Brompton Manor ended when Lady Brompton rose and gestured to her.

"We will retire to the drawing room for our tea and wait for the gentlemen to join us."

"Ladies," the earl of Brompton said as Lady Brompton and Amilie prepared to depart, but Lord Brompton's attention was riveted on Fitzhugh. "We shall have our port, and, at long last, I will enjoy a gentleman's conversation. Been surrounded too long by women who order me about and physicians who dose me with nasty remedies." Lord Brompton threw back his head and laughed heartily until his laughter turned into spasms of coughing.

"Brompton. You are forbidden to overtax yourself this evening."

"I shall charge Fitzhugh with keeping my merriment contained. Now, the two of you hurry off before your tea cools."

As soon as Amilie and Lady Brompton were out of earshot the earl of Brompton leaned toward his ward.

"So Fitzhugh, you have resigned your commission and now find yourself at loose ends. What do you intend?"

"I am considering the church. Serving a parish should be to my liking."

The earl sputtered and coughed into his handkerchief. He motioned to a footman.

"Fitzhugh lend a hand here. I feel my strength beginning to ebb, a return to the comfort of the dower house and my bed will be the wise course."

Braced by Fitzhugh on one side and a footman on the other, the earl of Brompton rose from the chair with a grunt.

"Give the ladies my apology for not joining them in the drawing room, and tell my dearest wife I shall spend my night anticipating her morning visit."

Holding an empty teacup in her hand, Lady Brompton peered across the tea service at Amilie. "I have inquired into the condition of your wardrobe. The dress you are wearing is most becoming, but tomorrow I shall make arrangements for the services of a mantua-maker."

Amilie set down her teacup. "Your ladyship, your offer is generous and well-taken, but I shall be happy to spare you the expense of a mantua-maker. I am talented with a needle and have constructed my clothing for several years now."

"But, my dear child, so many new items are needed.

A mantua-maker is necessary if you are to have a proper wardrobe finished in time."

Amilie drew in air and held her breath as she tried to discern the meaning of Lady Brompton's words. She did not dare ask what was meant by 'finished in time.' Nor for what occasions she would need so many new items.

Picking up her teacup she accepted the offer of more tea. "Perhaps a seamstress to fashion a riding habit for my lessons and a ball gown in the event I am invited to attend a ball."

Lady Brompton lowered her tea cup. "And morning dresses and afternoon dresses and dinner dresses and carriage dresses. All with matching accessories."

A tear spilled from the corner of Amilie's eye and trickled down the side of her cheek. The thought of living in a manner that required such an extensive wardrobe frightened her.

"I believe my response to your offer of abundance is damped by the modesty of my upbringing. So many dresses for so many occasions . . ." Amilie opened the small, evening reticule that matched her dress and fished about for her handkerchief.

"Dry your tears before the gentlemen come in, Amilie. I did not realize an offer of new dresses would be so upsetting to you. We will start with a riding habit and a new dinner dress in a shade of green flattering to your eyes, if you wish."

Amilie nodded and took in a deep breath. "My mother . . ."

The sound of the loud, rapid clicks of approaching boot heels caught her ear. Before she could complete her sentence, Fitzhugh strode into the drawing room, filling the room with his energy and covering the distance between the door and the area where she and Lady Brompton were seated in record time. "My dear ladies, I am instructed to inform you Lord Brompton has returned to the dower house. He extends his sincere regrets."

Lady Brompton leaned forward in her seat. Her brow furrowed, her eyes registering concern. "Brompton was in your charge, Fitzhugh. You were to keep him from overdoing."

"I failed."

"Should I go to him?"

"Lord Brompton said to inform you he is fine, only overset from such a historic night. He looks forward to your visit in the morning."

Lady Brompton sat back in her chair, dropped her shoulders and wrung her hands. "Brompton was too lively tonight. His excitement over your return and meeting his granddaughter for the first time made him eager to dine at table tonight. Since becoming ill, he has taken comfort being surrounded by his mother's things in the smaller dower house. Perhaps he put too much strain on his returning strength by coming here for dinner."

Fitzhugh sat down. Amilie was mesmerized by his smile and his sparkling eyes. She had never seen a man so enticingly handsome.

"Lord Brompton's happiness over my return came nowhere near matching the joy of meeting his grand-daughter for the first time. He spent a good bit of time wiping his eyes, blowing his nose and exclaiming about her charms before he asked the first question about my misadventures."

Lady Brompton's voice sounded far away to Amilie. "I should have known seeing the two of you at table to-night would overset him."

Lady Brompton stood. Fitzhugh and Amilie got to their feet. "I expect you in my dressing room at the ap-pointed time tomorrow, Amilie."

"Your Ladyship. I look forward to the morning."

Lady Brompton bade the two young people good-night, her face a web of distress.

Amilie made her curtsy, Fitzhugh his bow.

The two remained standing until Lady Brompton exited the drawing room. The hall footman took up a position inside the room, standing to one side of the open doors.

Amilie and Fitzhugh sat across from one another, eyeing each other with a sudden shyness.

"I would welcome a cup of tea, Miss Jasperton."

"I am remiss in my duties, Mr. Fitzhugh." Amilie picked up an unused teacup and filled it with tea. "Milk or lemon, sir?"

"Lemon. A hint of tartness in my tea fits my mood."

After several sips, he lowered the cup and gazed at Amilie with a sober face and clouded eyes. "How are you faring here, Miss Jasperton?"

"I am feeling lost, Mr. Fitzhugh. I have only the vaguest idea of the direction to take to return me to my apartments."

"This ancient house mystifies even me with its nooks and crannies and twists and turns." Fitzhugh said slapping his knee and roaring with laughter.

Amilie's hand jerked at his unexpected outburst. Tea sloshed from her cup into the saucer.

"When you are ready to go upstairs, you need only summon a footman to escort you, Miss Jasperton."

"And how does one summon a footman, Mr. Fitzhugh?"

"Ah. You are not familiar with the workings of these old piles of stone, I see."

"A vicar and his family live in far more humble accommodations. One can find one's way about a vicarage within minutes of entering and with no need of a footman for escort."

Fitzhugh nodded as his expression sobered. "Many who chose the work of the church find themselves in limited circumstances. I contemplate joining them."

"Do you Mr. Fitzhugh? My father found great joy in his work in spite of the limitations on his earnings. He had a fine intellect, a keen humor. My mother matched him in intellect and humor." Amilie blinked back the tears that once again filled her eyes. "They loved me dearly, Mr. Fitzhugh."

"I am sure they did, Miss Jasperton. I offer my condolences."

Amilie straightened her shoulders. "Now, I should

like to return to my apartments and would appreciate your showing me how I might summon the footman for escort."

Fitzhugh untangled his long legs, moved to the wall and pulled a bell chord near the chimneypiece. "There is a bell chord in every room, Miss Jasperton. In large rooms, there are sometimes two. They are tied to a clapper and when pulled, the clapper is posed to strike a bell on the bell box below stairs. The clang of the bell alerts the footman on duty that service is needed and the room in which it is required."

"How very clever. Perhaps a bell chord should be hung in the courtyard for people who need the service of a groom."

"You heard my shouts, Miss Jasperton?" The amused sparkle had returned to Fitzhugh's eyes.

"My apartments front on the entrance courtyard. Your shouts jarred me out of a deep sleep."

"My apologies." Fitzhugh executed a deep bow. When he straightened up, his eyes crackled with silent laughter. "I see your parents passed their humor and their intellect on to you, Miss Jasperton."

Before she thought of something to say in response, the summoned footman appeared in the doorway.

"Goodnight, Mr. Fitzhugh," she called as she headed for the room's exit.

When Amilie entered her sitting room, she found Helaine dozing in one of the wing chairs.

"You look tired, miss." Helaine said as she got to her feet. "I've kept a pitcher of water warm by the fire. Do you wish my help to prepare for bed?"

The mantle clock chimed the hour of nine.

"Help me out of my dress and loosen my hair. Then you may go. I shall wash my face and get to bed at once. Lady Brompton expects me in her dressing room tomorrow morning at ten.

Helaine began undoing the fastenings on Amilie's dress. "Was his lordship in good spirits this evening, miss?"

"He was very lively at dinner, but did not join us after for tea."

"I pray for his full recovery, miss."

"And I too. He is nothing like the stern gentleman I imagined he would be."

Chapter Four

Amilie arrived at the dressing room at ten as instructed and waited for the countess of Brompton to make her appearance.

The room was quiet. Amilie's idle thoughts gave rise to more questions. If she was invited to remain here in the care of the earl and countess of Brompton, titled people whom she would not have recognized in public and of whom she knew little, would she stay? And if she did, what would her future be like? The offer of dancing lessons and riding lessons excited her. But what was expected of her in return was not clear.

The woman who announced the countess of Brompton the previous day entered the dressing room. When Amilie asked Helaine who she was, Helaine told her the woman served as lady's maid to Lady Brompton.

"Miss Jasperton, her ladyship will be delayed this

morning. Please take a seat." The woman retreated through the door closing it behind her.

Amilie sat down on the same slipper chair she had sat in the previous day and began a closer examination of the paintings on the walls. On the far wall a portrait of a young woman caught her eye. She rose from her chair, moved closer and tilted her head back to peer upward.

Amilie felt her heart give a flutter. The young woman in the painting mimicked the reflection she saw when she looked in a looking-glass. The brunet hair with red highlights, the round, green eyes, the heart-shaped face, the full lips, all looked familiar. Amilie crossed her hands atop her chest to cover her heart. The woman in the portrait was her mother. After all the years of their estrangement, her mother's likeness still hung on the wall in the dressing room of the woman who had banished her.

"A great beauty, your mother," a pensive voice said from behind her.

Amilie turned to face Lady Brompton who stood in the open doorway between the two rooms.

"And you have been blessed with her beauty, Amilie."

Amilie pivoted her head to study the painting again. "I thank you, your ladyship." She turned her eyes away from the painting and made her curtsy. "I never thought of myself as beautiful. My father placed great value on a charitable and honest character. His concern was with the state of my character, and I fear I needed his reminder at times."

"One's good character is considered of high value in

this home too, Amilie. But fulfilling one's duty that attaches to privilege carries a higher value. So many depend on Brompton's benevolence and good stewardship that if he should choose not to honor his obligation to duty, they would suffer greatly."

Amilie made no response. The burdens carried by peers were mysterious to her. But her father carried many burdens too—for the souls of his parishioners and for the general welfare of the parish. Perhaps neither an earl's life nor a vicar's life was easy.

Lady Brompton sat down and gestured to the chair across from her. "Be seated, Amilie. I wish to go over a few things with you." Her voice was commanding, her tone brisk. "I have scheduled your riding lessons. They begin tomorrow morning. Helaine will show you to the riding ring to meet with the groom at nine o'clock."

Amilie grasped the sides of her chair. "A gentle horse, I should hope. My experience with horses is limited. I am somewhat leery of them."

Lady Brompton drew herself into a regal posture. "The selection of a horse and your riding instruction will be handled by Brompton's head groom. He will make a proper selection from our stables."

Amilie's gush of words refused to be contained. "My apology for speaking out of turn, your ladyship, but the thought of being atop a horse for the first time is thrilling and scary."

Lady Brompton's posture relaxed, her eyes warmed. "I was three the first time I sat atop a horse with my father. Over the years, I became exceedingly fond of riding. But I curtailed my daily ride when Brompton's health took a downturn."

Lady Brompton drew in a long breath and got to her feet. "One last item for today, Amilie. Helaine's advancement to the position of lady's maid to you needs only your approval."

Amilie gave Lady Brompton a broad smile. "Helaine is a wonderful choice. The duties of a lady's maid are not at all clear to me, but Helaine is given my approval."

Lady Brompton laughed a deep-throated chortle. "I forget, my dear Amilie, so many things here would most likely not be familiar to you. Helaine was born here. She knows this house and the people here as well as anyone. Her mother served us well for many years, and she will serve you well."

"And I like her a great deal. She is drawing maps of the interior of the Manor house for me to use until I learn my way about."

"A grand idea. Perhaps Brompton should hire a cartographer to draw up maps for issue to all of our guests. The Manor house has been added to and rearranged so often it has become a maze. Our guests, even those who have been here many times, are reluctant to step outside their bedchambers without a guide. When the house is full of visitors, our footmen are overextended."

Amilie joined in the laughter, the tense muscles in her shoulders relaxed as a sense of well-being pushed out her fears.

"Is there anything you wish to discuss with me, Amilie, before I leave?"

Amilie hesitated, rolling her eyes upward, she glanced at her mother's portrait—she dared not ask the questions she wanted answered. The answers might shatter her newfound feeling of ease.

Amilie returned her eyes to her hands in her lap. Twining her fingers around one another, she inhaled deeply. "It is a lovely day today. May I have permission to walk to the village? I noticed, when I passed through the village on my way here, several shops are available there. I have a few coins left after purchasing my coach ticket, and I have need of a new needlework canvas."

"You have my permission, but there is no need to walk. A carriage can be arranged to transport you wherever you wish to go."

"Thank you, your ladyship. I should enjoy a nice walk and am used to getting where I wish to go on foot."

Lady Brompton stood and gazed down at Amilie for several seconds before she spoke again.

"It is a lovely day. If Helaine accompanies you, you may walk to the village with my blessing. Exercise in the fresh air is always valued for good health and good spirits."

Amilie mused aloud. "Perhaps new trim for my bonnet instead of a canvas would be a better choice."

"My dearest child, purchase what you need or what catches your fancy. Helaine will introduce you to the shopkeepers and all the shops in the village carry a tab for Brompton Manor."

"A kind and generous offer, your ladyship, but I am able to pay for my purchases. My father's retirement fund has been invested and provides me a small yearly income."

"Do as you wish, but the shopkeepers' will be dismayed."

"Dismayed?"

"They depend on people buying their goods to support their families and the more a shopkeeper sells, the more his family prospers. Brompton Manor purchases a great deal of the local shops' inventory. They would expect the earl of Brompton's granddaughter to increase their sales several times over."

"It is not my intent to disappoint anyone, but spending my limited coins with abandon would not be a pleasure to me."

"Your need to maintain your independence is respected, Amilie. Enjoy your trip to the village. Come to my dressing room tomorrow morning at eleven. I wish to hear about your first riding lesson, and would enjoy seeing the purchases you make today."

When Lady Brompton turned and left the room, her lady's maid entered to inform Amilie a footman waited outside the hall door and would show her back to her apartments.

Amilie rushed through the door to her sitting room, eager to inform Helaine she had been approved as lady's maid. But Helaine was not in the sitting room and a check of the bedchamber showed she was not there either. Amilie sat down to read until Helaine returned, but the book lay unopened in her lap.

The second Helaine came through the door with a tray, Amilie announced her news. "Your promotion to lady's maid is arranged. Helaine."

"Yes, miss." A grin lighted up Helaine's face. The housekeeper gave me the news only moments ago." Helaine set a tray with Amilie's lunch dishes on the table. "It will be my honor to serve you, miss." She dropped a curtsy.

"And I am fortunate to have you in that position. Your counsel has already served me well."

Amilie sat down at the table and eyed the dishes sent up for her lunch. She looked over at Helaine who was engaged in inspecting the room.

"We are to make a visit to the village this afternoon. I have been given permission by Lady Brompton. We will travel on foot."

Helaine turned to face Amilie. "Carriages are available, miss."

"It is a beautiful day, no rain clouds await overhead, and I enjoy the slow pace of being on foot."

"Yes, miss."

Amilie took a bite of a cold meat pie and swallowed. "Forgive me, Helaine. I did not ask if you are able to cover the distance on foot. Please feel free to say if you are not."

"My comfort is not your concern, miss. I serve at your bidding. However, getting to the village on foot will not be difficult for me. When the weather is nice, rambling over these hills for hours is how I spend my free time."

"Your comfort is of my concern, Helaine. And you may ask permission to express your misgivings or difficulties at anytime."

"Enjoy your lunch, miss. I will return at half past the hour with my cloak and bonnet."

Amilie hurried through her lunch and stood at the window looking down the lawns to the road. Shadow and light danced together along the lane. The water of the lake sparkled with golden tints. Was her mother given a choice before her banishment? And if she were, what had her mother valued so highly she gave up the comforts and pleasure of Brompton Manor and all connection to her family?

Amilie sat down in the chair by the fire and indulged in a releasing crying spell until she heard her clock chime the half hour.

Wiping her cheeks and blowing her nose, she moved from the sitting room into her bedchamber, took down her bonnet, and regarded the trim.

"Miss?" Helaine called.

"I am here, Helaine." Amilie ran her finger across her cheeks one last time and tied on her bonnet.

She crossed the sitting room. "I shall purchase new trim for my bonnet today," she said to Helaine. "It is time I replace the black ribbons and the black edging."

"There is a lovely shop in the village which has a fine selection of trimmings. The proprietor of the shop goes to great effort to offer all that is the fashion in London."

"How lovely, but I fear what is fashionable in London would be too dear for the depth of my pocket."

"But. . . ." Helaine paused. ". . . perhaps you will set the fashion here, miss."

Amilie adjusted her bonnet, tied the ribbons tighter, and took her coins from a drawer in her writing desk. "I only intend to replace the mourning trim on my bonnet, Helaine. Setting the fashion here is of no interest to me."

Once they were outside, Amilie and Helaine moved along at a good pace. The air was stirred by a light breeze. The sun was warm without being overheating.

There was little traffic on the road—only an occasional cart or packhorse passed them as they strolled in the direction of the village.

"Our village has prospered from the new woolen mill," Helaine offered as she and Amilie passed the Duck and Quail Pub. "Several new shops have opened, and the confectioner has expanded his space and his offerings."

"I pray I shan't be tempted beyond my ability to pay."

"But, miss, if I may be bold, his lordship's household is extended credit at the shops. They will add your purchases."

"I know, Helaine. I received permission to purchase whatever catches my fancy, but I could not enjoy being extravagant. I have sufficient to purchase what I need."

"I see."

"Perhaps I may decide that a simpler life than the life at Brompton Manor is more suited to me. It may be I shall only be here for a short time. And since I have no desire to find myself in debtor's gaol, it is good to keep my feet planted in the earth and my head below the clouds."

"I see, miss." Helaine's eyes glistened. Her voice sounded muted and flat.

Nearing the mercer's shop, Helaine brightened. "You will find a good selection of fabric and trim here, miss."

Helaine pulled open the door of the shop. A bell jangled. A man came from the back room to greet them.

"The earl of Brompton's granddaughter, Miss Jasperton," Helaine announced to the mercer.

"I am delighted to have you honor my shop with your presence, Miss Jasperton. I am in recent receipt of a shipment from London that contained the most beautiful silks I have seen for sometime." He moved a bolt of pale pink silk to the counter and held out a length for Amilie's inspection.

"It is a lovely fabric, Mr. White, but today my interest is in purchasing new trim for my bonnet."

"You are fortunate. My order to London for the latest, most fashionable ribbons and trims arrived yesterday."

"Perhaps some trim from your older stock."

Mr. White's face soured for a moment, but the downturn of his eyes and lips was soon replaced by his earlier lively countenance.

"Of course. There is still some fine older stock available. If you are disposed to wait a moment, I will retrieve the box from the back."

Eyeing the colorful bolts of fabric stacked against the far wall, Amilie spotted a large basket sitting atop a rear counter and began to sort through the contents. A length of burgundy ribbon, long enough to replace her bonnet ribbons, and a burgundy and pink silk flower caught her eye.

"Helaine, these are lovely . . . ," she said, holding them out for inspection, ". . . and greatly reduced in price."

Amilie noticed Helaine's jaw drop.

Before she could ask the reason, Mr. White emerged from the back carrying a lidded box. Speaking with great enthusiasm, he began praising the quality of the wares inside.

"Mr. White, I have found the perfect trim and at an excellent bargain."

Mr. White covered his mouth, coughing a dry cough. He placed the box he was carrying on the counter. "I am delighted you have found something to your liking in my humble shop, Miss Jasperton."

Amilie opened her reticule, took out her coin purse and laid the correct amount on top of the counter.

"Your shop is filled with beautiful things, Mr. White. I look forward to patronizing your fine establishment many times in the future."

The proprietor's face lighted up. A grin brightened his face. "It is my pleasure to serve you at any time, Miss Jasperton. If you wish a particular item ordered from London, it will be my pleasure to handle the transaction for you."

Amilie thanked the proprietor and complimented him on his lovely wares once more before leaving.

Back on the footpath, she and Helaine strolled along the line of shops. Amilie examined the goods displayed in the windows, and chattered away with excitement about her purchase and about the goods in the shop windows. She lingered in front of the local milliner's, making a close examination of a bonnet.

"The shops here are full of temptation, Helaine. I must stop looking at everything. If there is a stationery shop nearby, I should like to visit. And I should like to inquire about purchasing a subscription at the library."

"There is the stationer's shop around the bend and a short distance along. It sits right next to the confectioner's shop. The subscription library is up ahead and across the street."

"Then we will stop at the library first unless you are tired."

"I am not at all tired, miss." Helaine pulled out her timepiece and studied the hands. "There will be time enough to dress for dinner if we start our return within the half hour, miss."

Amilie and Helaine continued on, no longer dallying to examine the shop windows. When they were directly across from the subscription library, they paused at the curb to check for oncoming carts or horses.

"Miss Jasperton," Mr. Fitzhugh's distinctive voice exclaimed.

Amilie's breath caught, she heard a loud gasp and realized she had sounded it. Her arms crossed over her heart as she pivoted in time to see Fitzhugh step the rest of the way through the door of the shop directly behind them.

"Mr. Fitzhugh. Forgive me. Your unexpected greeting startled me. In a village in which I am a stranger, I did not expect to hear my name called." Amilie glanced at the sign over the doorway of the shop from which he emerged. "I see we both have come into the village today to refresh our wardrobes."

Fitzhugh tipped his hat. "Miss Jasperton, a pleasure to see you in our splendid village this afternoon. I was in dire need of some good English tailoring. America is greatly lacking in the quality of their tailoring."

Amilie managed a smile, though his sudden appearance had left her feeling breathless. "I should like to hear of your experiences in America," Amilie said stepping back, thankful her heartrate was slowing.

"My pleasure, Miss Jasperton. Is there a carriage waiting for you?"

"We are on foot."

"Then, if I am given your permission, I shall leave my horse at the stables and join you on your return to the Manor." He looked at her with a wry smile on his face. "I hope you do not think me weak for riding such a short distance."

Amilie laughed, forgetting her desire to stop at the subscription library and the stationery shop. She fell into step with Mr. Fitzhugh as he started in the direction of Brompton Manor. Helaine followed close behind.

Chapter Five

Fitzhugh's long stride kept moving him ahead of Amilie as they walked along. Each time he halted until she caught up and attempted to adjust the length of his stride to hers.

"Tell me when I am going too fast, Miss Jasperton. I fear I tend to hurry more than is necessary."

"And I tend to dawdle, Mr. Fitzhugh. At times, I am so caught up in my thoughts I find myself barely moving at all and end up arriving at my destination long after the intended time."

"Then I propose I learn to slow down and you learn to speed up. A good compromise that could benefit us both, Miss Jasperton."

Amilie laughed merrily. "Perhaps we shall influence one another in other ways too. All to the good, Mr. Fitzhugh."

The two strolled along in an amiable silence at a middling speed.

"Are you feeling more settled, Miss Jasperton?"

"I am. Helaine has been assigned as lady's maid to me. Her presence and knowledge of things has eased my way a great deal. She is drawing up maps of the interior of the Manor house for me so I am able to find my way without an escort."

"Or a need to search for the bell chords."

"Exactly, Mr. Fitzhugh," Amilie said with laughter in her voice.

He turned his head to the side. "Helaine and I grew up together at Brompton Manor." He leaned toward Amilie and cupped his hand next to his mouth. "Helaine has a fine character and a big heart," he said in a loud whisper. "And she does not hesitate to point out the errors of one's ways. I fear she read me many a scold over the years."

"Only to save you from yourself, Mr. Fitzhugh," Helaine said from behind them.

A big grin split Fitzhugh's face, plumping his angular cheeks. He returned his attention to Amilie. "Youthful daring landed me in bumble broth more than once."

"And to aid your tutor, who found himself constantly at wit's end and pleading with me to find where you got off to," Helaine added.

Fitzhugh threw back his head and laughed a hearty laugh. "You see what you are to contend with, Miss Jasperton?"

Amilie looked back at Helaine. "You may relax,

Helaine. I promise to give no one reason to find their self at wit's end."

"Thank you, miss."

Amilie half-skipped a few steps to catch up with Fitzhugh. "Tell me about the rash deeds your youthful enthusiasms led you to engage in, Mr. Fitzhugh."

He looked down at Amilie and smiled an enchanting smile. The expression in his eyes resembled the expression of every mischievous young lad about to embark on an adventure.

"I loved to climb—the higher the better—and once fell from a tree, resulting in numerous scrapes and bruises, even a small gash in my arm. Helaine found me huddled beneath the tree, holding my arm and moaning. She took me back to the house, covered the scrapes with ointment and stuck a court-plaster on the gash all the while chastising me."

Fitzhugh chuckled and kicked at a stone in the road sending it skittering along the surface.

"Then there was the day I challenged myself to hunt down and capture the gander who roamed the grounds. The gander wanted no part of my game and protested my attempts by flapping his powerful wings at a furious rate, coming straight at me and nipping me with his beak. Fortunately, Helaine came along in time. The old gander responded to her as though she was his mother, instantly obeying her command to cease his attack. After she shooed him off, she escorted me to the stillroom and dabbed my open wounds with a stinging tincture. A painful misadventure."

Amilie laughed with more delight than she had for some time. "I am comforted to know I am served well with Helaine as lady's maid."

Fitzhugh bent his head closer to Amilie's ear and spoke in a low voice. "Trust Helaine. Her service to you will be vigilant and loyal." Fitzhugh raised his head and looked down the road. "And your behavior when a youth, Miss Jasperton?"

"I am afraid docile and circumspect describe my behavior. As the daughter of a vicar, my actions were always of interest to members of the parish. The spinsters and the childless widows kept their eyes trained on me at all times. I never wanted my behavior to reflect poorly on my parents."

"And you never longed for freedom from the strictures imposed on you as the child of a vicar?"

"I am free of any restraints now, Mr. Fitzhugh. And my freedom is not a happy state."

Fitzhugh stopped walking and took Amilie's elbow in his hand to stop her forward movement. "My sincere apologies, Miss Jasperton. Losing your parents is the cruelest of losses. My words were thoughtless."

Amilie gazed into Fitzhugh's sobered, contrite face, and blinked several times to hold back her ever-present tears.

"You need not make your apologizes, Mr. Fitzhugh. My situation has been known to you for only a short time."

"A most grievous lapse on my part, Miss Jasperton.

The black trim on your bonnet is indication to anyone but an unsighted man that you are in mourning."

"My visit to the shops in the village today was undertaken to purchase new trimmings. The sadness over the loss of my parents will be a part of me forever, but it is time to end my public mourning and search for a new purpose and a new joy in my life."

The rest of the way back to the Manor house Amilie and Fitzhugh restricted their conversation to comments about the weather and the things they took notice of along the road.

Nearing the entrance door of Brompton Manor, Amilie remarked on how much faster the distance had been covered on her return trip.

"You see, Miss Jasperton. With my good influence, you have begun moving at a faster pace already."

"So fast we failed to talk of your adventures in America. I am curious to learn the news about our ex-colony, and I look forward to hearing of your experience there."

Fitzhugh's eyelids descended, his lips thinned. "One day I shall speak to you of the occasion for my being there. My experiences in America are complicated and require a lengthy explanation."

"Then a time convenient," Amilie said as, single file, the three moved through the wide doorway and into the Manor house.

Fitzhugh bowed, made his *adieus*, and set off toward the rear section of the ground floor.

"I believe I am capable of finding my apartments from here, Helaine."

"The maps are finished, miss. If you wish to wait in the blue drawing room, I will return with them shortly."

Amilie strolled around the small blue drawing room while she waited for Helaine's return. She peered at the porcelain figurines, studied the paintings and portraits on the walls, and touched the delicate fabrics in the room while reliving her encounter with Mr. Fitzhugh. He was an entertaining and energetic gentleman. His actions and outward demeanor made him appear untroubled, but she sensed, in the depths of his soul, he harbored a profound loneliness that matched her own.

Sitting down in an armless chair, upholstered in blue damask, Amilie smoothed her fingers along the fabric that covered the sides of the seat. Her eyes moved upward and studied the painted ceiling. The artist depicted fat, smiling cherubs and reclining females draped in thin fabric with handsome males attending them.

The thought Mr. Fitzhugh would have been an apt model for the male figures in the ceiling tableau made her face warm. She closed her eyes and did not open them until she had lowered her head toward the floor. Once she could no longer see the ceiling she opened them again; she studied the floral patterns in the rug.

"My apologies for taking so long to return, miss." Helaine's breaths were coming in short gasps as she dropped a deep curtsy.

"I hardly noticed the time, Helaine. A close exami-

nation of the beautiful items in this room made me unaware of the number of minutes ticking by."

"Yes, miss. Cook stopped me to tell me the his lordship is ailing and dinner is being served in individual
apartments. Then the housekeeper stopped me and inquired about extra things needed in your apartments
and. . . ."

"Your delay is of no concern, Helaine."

Helaine dropped a second deep curtsy and held up a
thick packet of folded papers. "The maps, miss. I drew
a map of each floor, including below stairs and the attics, on a separate sheet of paper."

"Since dinner is not being served in the dining room
tonight, I will use the time to study your maps. Perhaps
tomorrow my exploration of each of the floors can begin." Amilie took the packet of folded paper from
Helaine.

"If I may, miss. Below stairs is the servants' domain
and many of the staff have rooms in the attics. It would
be best not to explore either on your own."

"I appreciate your caution, Helaine. Intruding on the
servants' privacy is not my desire."

"The housekeeper will arrange a time for you to visit
below stairs, and I will notify the staff before a tour of
the attics is made."

Amilie took the map with ground floor printed in
block letters across the bottom edge of the paper and
studied the drawing. She turned the sheet of paper to
orient the map to her current position. "This is an ex-

cellent depiction, Helaine. Now I am off. Check upstairs in a half-hour to learn if I am in my sitting room," Amilie started off with a wave of her hand. Peels of her merry laughter hung in the air as she hurried from the drawing room.

Amilie opened the door to her sitting room, leaned her back against her closed door and sighed with relief. She had taken only one wrong turn and had easily made a correction in her route using Helaine's maps.

She moved into her bedchamber and stowed all her outdoor things in their proper place except for her bonnet. She took her sewing kit from the drawer and, untying the string from her purchase, opened the package of trim and arranged everything on a small table next to one of the wing chairs. Settling down in the chair, Amilie picked up her scissors, closed her eyes and offered up a prayer. Opening her eyes, she cut through the first stitch holding the black ribbon outlining the brim. She snipped at the threads with care to avoid damaging the bonnet itself, until none of the black edging remained, then removed the ribbons. Neatly folding the separated pieces, she wrapped them in paper and placed them in her mother's keepsake box. Then she began to stitch on her new burgundy trim.

Half-an-hour passed. Helaine entered from the hall carrying a small tea tray. "You found your way here without becoming lost, miss?"

"A wrong turn at the top of the stairs, but I checked your maps and realized my error before going far."

"Very good, miss. Since tonight's supper will be

lighter than expected, Cook has free space on the stove and is heating enough bath water for everyone."

"What a splendid luxury. I shall take advantage of the opportunity for a bath. Have a tub and water brought as soon as they are available." Amilie rose to her feet to examine the treats Helaine had brought on the tea tray. "I thought I heard a pensive note in the earl's conversation last evening," she said picking up a macaroon. "His stories about his shooting parties greatly amused him, but there was an undertone of sorrow beneath his recollections."

Helaine nodded her head. "In years past, before he fell ill, the rooms of Brompton Manor were filled with guests. The moment Parliament ended its session his lordship did not linger in town. Once he returned here, it would not be long before the carriages of his lordship's guests would begin to arrive in great number. He misses the activity."

"What is the prognosis for his ailment?" Amilie asked after taking a sip of the hot, fragrant tea.

"The butler has told the staff the doctors are hopeful."

"And why does he stay at the dower house?"

"I believe his lordship takes comfort in the smaller rooms of the dower house. Several times, I heard his lordship speak with fondness of the gardens there. When his mother, the dowager countess was alive, she lived there. Her passion became the gardens surrounding the dower house. His lordship has everything kept exactly the same as when she lived there."

Amilie sat back down in the wing chair and picked

up her bonnet. Concentrating on her stitches, she tried to erase the vision of her mother kneeling in the dirt to tend the flowers and vegetables in the garden behind the vicarage.

Helaine disappeared into the bedchamber; minutes later she re-entered the sitting room and spoke softly. "Your tea is growing cold, miss."

Amilie raised her head and gazed into the fireplace for a moment, then put her sewing aside and rose to her feet.

"I will sit by the window, finish my tea while I wait for the bathwater."

"Yes, miss."

Amilie stood beside one of the tall windows holding the teacup in her hand. She scanned the vista spread before her. Brompton Manor offered her so many opportunities. Exploring the beautiful things in the house and the surrounding grounds, discovering delightful surprises within and without, her riding lessons, learning the dance steps, and attending balls where well-dressed and mannered gentleman would request to partner her.

She should not have told Fitzhugh she was docile and compliant while growing up; he would think her uninteresting. She should have said she satisfied her longing for adventure by reading. It would have been a better description of her as a youth. Docile and circumspect sounded dull.

Early the next morning, Helaine led Amilie to an enclosed, riding ring. The groom stood inside the fence holding the reins and patting the neck of a chestnut mare. The mare stood quietly, swishing her tail or blinking an eye on occasion. The horse appeared calm and steady. Amilie took the small pome the groom held out to her. At his direction, she placed the fruit in the palm of her hand and held it up to the mare. As the horse nuzzled the pome from her hand, the soft, warm touch of the mare's nose and lips surprised and delighted her.

"She is beautiful. What is her name?"

"Shining Star, miss."

The groom pointed to a block inserted into the ground beside the mare. "Step up on the block with your left foot, miss, and swing up into the saddle."

Amilie followed the groom's instructions and to her delight found herself seated in the sidesaddle. The saddle was not as tipsy as she imagined it would be when she saw the ladies of the squire's family riding by the vicarage. In fact, the saddle fit comfortably, although her position strained any sense of familiarity.

She looked around. She could see a great distance seated up here. And in the near distance, the unmistakable figure of Mr. Fitzhugh was heading in the direction of the riding ring. His long stride got him to the fence outside the riding ring seconds later.

"Good Morning, Miss Jasperton. I had no idea you were riding today . . . ," he said as he leaned against the white fence, ". . . until I heard the news in the stables.

"Today is my first lesson, Mr. Fitzhugh. And I am happy to report I feel confident sitting atop this splendid horse."

"I gave Shining Star her name. It was apparent to me when she foaled she was a horse with a special destiny."

"Foretelling the future is a talent of yours, Mr. Fitzhugh?"

"Not really," Fitzhugh answered and laughed his hearty laugh. "Only about this mare. Everything else in my life has come upon me as a surprise. Now, on with your lesson, Miss Jasperton, I am off to retrieve my horse from the village stables."

The groom glowered at Fitzhugh at the mention of the village stables.

"The horse is being well cared for. I bribed the second stable boy," Fitzhugh called in his booming voice as he loped off toward the lane.

Holding Shining Star's reins, the groom began to lead the mare around the ring. "Settle back into the saddle, miss, and keep your back straight; try to move with the rhythm of the horse."

Amilie settled in, following the groom's instructions and quickly caught the movement of the mare's stride.

How wonderful it felt to move in rhythm with another living creature.

"Tomorrow you have the reins, miss," the groom said as he helped Amilie dismount.

"I look forward to tomorrow. All of my anxiety about horses is gone." Amilie patted Shining Star's neck. "She is a fine horse."

"Shining Star is a gentle lady, miss, well-behaved and responsive to commands."

"You were her trainer?"

" 'Twas, miss. She ain't ever been rid'n by a gentleman."

Amilie smiled at the groom's words. "Spared from the high spirits of Mr. Fitzhugh, I presume?"

The groom swiveled his head, his face obscured from Amilie's sight. And though the expression on his face was hidden, the loud snort that sounded affirmed her suspicion.

Amilie was smiling and giggling when she joined Helaine by the fence. She checked the hands of her watch. "It is nearing the time for my appointment with Lady Brompton. We best hurry."

"Yes, miss. I thought to call to you if your lesson went longer. Her ladyship is strict about people being on time."

"Then we are off at once, and we shall travel at Mr. Fitzhugh's pace," Amilie said. She set off with as long a stride as she was capable of. Helaine hurried to keep up.

Both Amilie and Helaine were gasping for breath and holding their sides as they entered Amilie's apartments. Helaine poured water into the washbasin. Amilie made a quick wash of her hands then peered into the toilette mirror attached to her washstand.

"I look glowing, Helaine."

"Yes, miss, the fresh air and your fast walk back to the Manor heightened your coloring."

Amilie glanced at Helaine's face. "And you benefited from the vigorous exercise too, Helaine. Your cheeks are as rosy as the upholstery fabric."

The color in Helaine's face deepened. She dipped

her head. "Miss, 'tis time you should change clothes and start for her ladyship's rooms."

With Helaine's help, Amilie got out of her riding outfit and into a sprigged muslin dress. Helaine wound a matching ribbon through Amilie's hair and stood back. "There, miss. Do you need me to lead the way this morning?"

"I shall find my way using your maps. Enjoy a cup of tea below stairs while I wander the hallways and have my visit with Lady Brompton."

Chapter Six

Amilie sat in the dressing room with her newly trimmed bonnet in her hand.

"You are flushed, child. Are you ill?"

"The stimulation of my first riding lesson has peaked my color."

"Riding is exceedingly rousing. It has been far too long since I have ridden. Now that Brompton is better, I shall have a long ride soon."

Amilie sat quietly as her breathing slowed and the stillness in the dressing room settled around her.

"Are you and Helaine getting on?"

"We are, your ladyship. The maps she drew for me are very precise and easy to follow. I should like a tour below stairs if arrangements can be made. Helaine has offered to show me through the attics once the servants are notified of a time."

"The housekeeper will be of help to you. I think you will find Brompton Manor is managed like any dwelling of its size. Now tell me of your visit to the village yesterday."

"The village and the shops are full of lovely things. I found a wonderful bargain at the mercer's shop and have sewn the new trim I purchased there on my bonnet."

Amilie held out the bonnet for inspection.

Lady Brompton took it from her and inspected the workmanship carefully. "Lovely, my dear. Your stitches are well-done and this burgundy was a wonderful choice of color. And what other purchases might you have made?"

"Nothing more. I did see lovely fabrics at the mercer's and a delightful bonnet in the milliner's window. We looked in the shop windows for a time and were about to cross the street to inquire at the subscription library when we encountered Mr. Fitzhugh. He offered to escort us on our return and so we did not tarry."

Amilie saw a flicker of interest flash in Lady Brompton's eyes as she handed back the bonnet.

"You are of an age to enjoy a gentleman's attentions." Lady Brompton's eyes intensified as she stared at Amilie for several long seconds.

Amilie squirmed under the pointed and assessing gaze.

"Be wise in your decisions, my child. Marriages last a long time. There can be sad consequences if one makes a wrong choice. Taking one's time to explore all possible suitors allows one to make the highest and the best marriage arrangement possible."

Amilie considered the words. She imagined there was a hidden message in them, but she had no idea what that message might be. Her parents spoke often of their good fortune in having met one another and married. She understood many marriages at the upper levels of society were arranged. And if what she read was true, love or a special affinity for one another appeared of no importance in such arrangements. But even though she understood this as true, she did not understand why it was so.

Lady Brompton stood. "Now, I am off for my daily visit to my darling Brompton. He waits impatiently for me to come at this hour every day. He informed me he desires a long talk with you as soon as he is stronger. Do take some time today to practice your music. Brompton is partial to Mozart."

"Then a renewal of my acquaintance with Mozart's music is in order," Amilie said rising and curtsying.

After Lady Brompton entered the adjoining room and closed the door, Amilie took out her maps and set her course for the music room. Turn right, then make a left at the next intersection of corridors and down the stairs to the first floor. Helaine did a grand job. Each room, on every floor, was labeled in neat block printing.

Amilie found the music room with no wrong turns.

The oval-shaped room contained dozens of armless, gilded chairs lined up, single file, against the walls—

their seats upholstered in shiny, red silk. A small stage rose above the floor at one end of the oval and a pianoforte sat to Amilie's left, right below the stage. She sat down at the musical instrument and fingered the keys. Her ears filled with the full, rich tone of the notes. She began to practice with zeal. Totally engrossed, she floated with the music.

She did not know how much time elapsed when she caught sight of Helaine standing beside the pianoforte. She looked up from the keys and stilled her fingers.

"I am to tell you tonight's dinner is being served in the dining room after all, miss. Her ladyship found his lordship in good spirits and eager to join the family at table tonight."

Amilie nodded and finished the last few bars of the piece she was practicing. "This is such a marvelous instrument. Finer than any I have been privileged to play before."

"You play well, miss."

"Music affords me a great deal of pleasure. Until I experienced being atop Shining Star, my greatest pleasure was my music."

"Same as his lordship, miss. We often enjoy musicians here and this room has been used many times for musical performances."

As they hurried to return to Amilie's apartments to get her ready for dinner, Amilie held up her hand with the folded maps. "Who printed the letters on your maps, Helaine?"

"Myself, miss. Mr. Fitzhugh taught me to read and write. He hated being cooped up in his schoolroom, and insisted we sit under the trees while he taught me my letters and then taught me to read. I grumbled about his making me repeat and repeat; but secretly, miss, I enjoyed my lessons."

"I am pleased you read and write, Helaine. At home, I tutored the village children who showed an interest in learning. Being literate opens the doors for a better future."

"Yes, miss. Mr. Fitzhugh taught me to cipher too. If I am to advance up the servant ranks to housekeeper, reading, writing, and ciphering are necessary. I owe a debt to Mr. Fitzhugh." Helaine's eyes widened for a moment. "Never let on to Mr. Fitzhugh I said so, miss."

Amilie no longer wondered about the easiness between Helaine and Fitzhugh. After his stories of Helaine's rescuing him from his mishaps and her confession of his persistence in seeing to her learning, Amilie understood the obvious fondness they carried for one another.

Helaine took Amilie's silk dress from the wardrobe. "I gave your dinner dress a press and a brushing."

Amilie closed her eyes as the dress was slipped over her head then thrust her arms into the sleeve openings. "I shall need a second dinner dress if I am expected to dress for dinner so often. Perhaps the pink silk, if it is not too dear."

"Yes, miss."

"Lady Brompton said nothing more about the arrival of a mantua-maker."

"I am skilled with a needle, miss, and could fashion a dress from the pink silk for you."

"Then I shall return to the village tomorrow to purchase the silk or another fabric if I do not have the price for the silk. I am skilled at sewing too."

Amilie pulled the sleeves of her dress into position. With Helaine's attention, the lace trim no longer hung limp or looked dingy. "With both of us applying our needles, a new dress could be completed within days."

"Yes, miss."

"Then we shall go to the mercer's tomorrow if there are no other plans for me and I am given permission."

Amilie's previous tension over finding herself in such an elaborate setting for dinner was missing on her second evening. For the first time since her arrival at Brompton Manor, her appetite awakened. She spooned large servings of several offerings onto her plate and picked up her fork to eat.

Fitzhugh was seated across the table in direct line of her eyesight. No candelabra blocked her view of him. Each time she raised her eyes from her plate, his black hair, curling about his forehead, his sea blue eyes, sparkling with energy, caused her stomach to churn. Instead of eating with enjoyment, Amilie found herself picking at the mounds of food on her plate.

The earl of Brompton focused his attention on her

several times during the meal—beaming at her and asking her perfunctory questions. But, like the previous evening, he dominated the conversation with his stories. Tonight he recited the history and the details of his ailment including a detailed description of the various treatments he had endured.

"The expectations of my full recovery are increasing every day," he announced at the end of the first course. "I expect my health is improved enough to go to London for the opening of Parliament."

The butler placed bowls of nuts and sweetmeats on the table.

"Splendid news, your lordship," Fitzhugh said, then wiped his mouth with his serviette, plucked a sugared nut from the epergne, and popped it into his mouth. "Your peers are eager to have your wise counsel once again. Several of them mentioned this when I stopped in London before traveling here."

The earl of Brompton cleared his throat several times before he spoke again. "My efforts have influenced many of the important decisions taken for the benefit of England in the past. I hate being absent when Parliament sits."

"Then Amilie and I are to prepare ourselves for London. The mantua-maker's arrival date is Monday of next week. That should give her enough time to complete several new outfits for myself and for Amilie before we leave."

Amilie placed her fork on her plate and stared at Lady Brompton. "We are to go to London?"

"Of course, my dear, I never miss the opportunity to enjoy London. Town is socially quieter now—a perfect time to introduce you to important members of the *ton* who might be about and to make our preparations for your come-out."

Amilie felt as though her breath was being squeezed out of her. "Please excuse me. I am not feeling well." She got to her feet and dashed from the room.

Lady Brompton sat without moving; Brompton stared at Lady Brompton; Fitzhugh emptied his two-thirds full wine glass in one gulp and refilled the glass.

After several seconds, Lady Brompton signaled the butler to her side. "Send one of the footmen to find Helaine. I wish to speak with her."

Amilie gave her sitting room door a shove. The slam of the door underlined her feeling of distress. She threw herself into one of the wing chairs by the fireplace and curled her arms and legs around into a protective bundle. *A come-out*?

Was this what happened to her mother? She had refused to have a come-out and was sent away forever?

Not likely. Such an event would not have been a foreign idea to her mother. *But, I know no one of the aristocracy and would be lost in the midst the young ladies and gentlemen who were brought up in a privileged world of money and status.*

And London? Thoughts of the crowds, the noise, leaden skies, beggars in the streets, all of the things she heard people say about Town depressed her to think about.

Amilie curled her arms and legs tighter to her body. "I will refuse to accompany them. I shall insist on remaining here where things move at a pace I am comfortable with and where there is quiet and fresh air." Perhaps, one day she would make the trip to London to see Hyde Park and the British Museum, but never for the purpose of being introduced to society.

The sitting room door hinges squeaked as Helaine pushed it open and entered with a tray. "Her ladyship thought you might enjoy some tea and a macaroon biscuit or two."

Amilie wiped a tear from her cheek and stayed curled up and silent.

"Did Mr. Fitzhugh say something to upset you?"

Amilie's "no" was muffled by the wing of the chair. Then she unfurled herself and sat on the chair proper, but with her elbows on her knees and her head bowed. "Mr. Fitzhugh acted a perfect gentleman. He totally involved himself in keeping his glass filled and minding his dinner. But when Lord Brompton mentioned he was well enough to attend the opening of Parliament, Lady Brompton mentioned the mantua-maker would arrive in plenty of time to complete several new outfits for her and for me by the time we left for London." Amilie looked up. Tears streamed down her face. "And then Lady Brompton said she would take the occasion to introduce me to society. And then she mentioned the planning of a come-out for me. I do not wish a come-out. Nor do I wish to go to London."

Amilie sniffed and sprang to her feet. "Since I shall refuse any introduction to the *ton*, there is no purpose of having a come-out."

Amilie stomped from one side of the room to the other then stopped in the middle of the room. "Helaine, retrieve my valises and begin packing my things. I have enough for the purchase of a coach ticket, and I have the word of the squire that I am welcome to return to his household at any time I wish. I am only sorry to leave you behind, Helaine."

"If I may be bold, miss."

Amilie looked at Helaine. "What is it you wish to say?"

"I wish to say, miss. Do not leave until you talk with her ladyship. Your recent loss may be muddling your thoughts."

Amilie bit her bottom lip and bowed her head. Her stomping had cleared her head. "At the very least, I owe Lady Brompton an apology for my abrupt departure from the dinner table. My behavior this evening was far from docile and circumspect. If I caused the earl of Brompton upset, I shall not forgive myself."

"I believe his lordship is fine, miss. He was in the drawing room carrying on about seeing old friends again."

Amilie lifted her chin and moved to sit at the writing desk. "After I write a note of apology to Lady Brompton, you may deliver it to her apartments while I write my notes of apology to Lord Brompton and Mr. Fitzhugh. Once you have delivered the note to Lady Brompton you are free the rest of the night. I will ring for a footman to deliver the notes to Lord Brompton and Mr. Fitzhugh." Amilie dipped a quill pen into the ink. The pen flew across the paper; her foot tapped the floor. She sanded her note, folded the paper and handed it to Helaine.

"I have included a request in my note for an audience at Lady Brompton's convenience," she said. "Leave the tea tray 'til morning. My appetite has returned."

"Yes, miss." A grin lighted Helaine's face. "Sleep well, miss, I will return in the morning to wake you in time for your riding lesson."

"Until morning, then."

After Helaine set off with the note, Amilie remained seated at her writing desk to finish her other notes. Then she took out a fresh sheet of paper, sharpened a fresh quill, and began a letter to the squire informing him she was doing well.

"Miss Jasperton you appear restored after your illness last evening," Fitzhugh said as he fell into step with Amilie as she and Helaine made their way to the riding ring.

"I am quite improved this morning, Mr. Fitzhugh. Your advice to me about Helaine proved true. And thoughts of being atop Shining Star calms one."

"There is nothing like a good ride to settle a person's thoughts."

"Are you planning to ride today?"

"My intention is to ask permission to observe how you and Shining Star get on."

"Of course you may, but with one promise. You must not comment on my mistakes or laugh at my awkwardness."

Fitzhugh's face took on an exaggerated soberness. "I promise to hold my tongue. At all cost."

"See that you do."

The groom nodded to the three young people as they approached the area where he waited. Fitzhugh held out his hand to assist Amilie onto the mounting block. Her gloved hand in his both steadied and unsettled her.

Seated on the horse, Amilie's spirits flew to new heights. She smoothed down her skirt and took the reins from the groom. The groom set the mare into motion and Amilie merged herself with the measured rhythm of the horse. The groom followed alongside as horse and rider circled the ring three times.

"By yourself, this time, miss."

Amilie's heart pounded against her chest as she and Shining Star circled the ring without the groom beside her—twice around, at a steady pace, without mishap. Amilie's confidence increased with each step.

The groom called out instructions for halting the mare and after the third time around, Amilie brought Shining Star to a stop. Fitzhugh rushed forward to assist her in her dismount.

"Splendid. Your seat is near perfect, Miss Jasperton." Fitzhugh's face pinked as he covered a dry cough,

"Atop a horse," he quickly added. "I look forward to riding the estate grounds with you to acquaint you with the best of the many riding trails Brompton Manor has to offer."

Amilie's heart was demanding to be let out of the confinement of her chest. Her heartbeat pounded in her ears, drowning out any other sounds. She knew her feet were on solid ground but something was shaking beneath them, her vision narrowly focused on the blurred outline of Mr. Fitzhugh.

"Miss Jasperton?"

The sound of his voice broke the spell. The clarity of her vision returned. The clucking sounds of a hen searching the ground by the fence reached her ears.

"I best be off, Mr. Fitzhugh. I thank you for your compliment and look forward to accepting your offer."

"And where best you be off to, Miss Jasperton?" Fitzhugh asked restraining her with a light touch on her arm.

"If permitted, Helaine and I intend to walk to the village this afternoon."

"My plans for today include being in the village. Join me at the confectioner's shop. Say around the hour of two o'clock?"

"Perhaps I shall, Mr. Fitzhugh. If I am able to complete my errands in time."

The sound of a horse's hoofs caused Amilie and Fitzhugh to turn their eyes toward the area of the stables.

The horse and rider stopped before them. Lady Brompton spoke from her seat atop a white gelding.

"I am pleased to learn your riding lessons are going well, Amilie. Your enthusiasm over your lessons has encouraged me to ride again. Perhaps we shall ride together before long."

"I look forward to joining you, your ladyship."

"You may drop the formal address, Amilie. Grandmama is appropriate from now on. I expect you in the blue drawing room today at a quarter past eleven."

Without waiting for a response, the countess of Brompton urged her horse into a trot and rode off in the direction of the lake.

Amilie tightened her lips and folded her hands together as she uttered a word she had never spoken before. "Grandmama."

"Lady Brompton is usually cool and reserved in her manner, Miss Jasperton. She has relaxed and warmed considerably since your arrival."

"I confide in you Mr. Fitzhugh, I have been intimidated by the luxury of the surroundings here. I am grateful for the permission to call her grandmama. I believe my hesitation over speaking honestly to her of my fears and of other matters will be eased now."

"Lady Brompton carries herself with dignity and a sense of command, but she is fine humored, a good listener, and a wise counselor."

Tears welled in Amilie's eyes. When they spilled down her cheeks, she accepted the handkerchief Mr. Fitzhugh pulled from his jacket, wiped her cheeks, and blew her nose.

"I find myself in tears more often than is usual for me, Mr. Fitzhugh. I have become a real water pot."

"A sudden upset always increases the amount of fluid in one's eyes," he replied in a softened voice.

Amilie looked into Fitzhugh's face, her heart quivered when she noticed the pain dulling his eyes, her finger burned where it brushed his hand when she took the handkerchief from him. Shaking her head, she forced a laugh.

"How gloomy we find ourselves on this beautiful day. Now, I am off to prepare for my trip to the village if I am permitted, Mr. Fitzhugh. If so, I hope to have my errands completed in time and join you at the confectioner's shop."

Fitzhugh grinned. Amusement darted back into his eyes. "I have an uncontrollable hunger for the confectioner's small cakes. I found nothing in America that came close to the quality or taste of those cakes. I look forward to your joining me for my indulgence, Miss Jasperton."

Chapter Seven

Amilie washed and changed out of her riding clothes then sat at her writing desk and began a letter to a friend from home. When the mantle clock struck a quarter to the eleventh hour, she set the unfinished letter aside, checked her hair and her dress in the long cheval glass in her bedchamber, then left her room. On her way downstairs she tried to form the proper words into a sentence. Words that would explain why the idea of a having a come-out or going to London or being introduced to the *ton* upset her so.

When she entered the blue drawing room, Lady Brompton was sitting by the windows looking out, still wearing her riding habit. A tea service was on a table in front of her. Amilie curtsied. "Lady . . . grandmama."

A smile broke the reserve of Lady Brompton's countenance. "Will you have tea, Amilie?"

"Please."

After the tea was poured, Lady Brompton held onto her cup without drinking. "I won't keep you Amilie, but I wanted to thank you for your timely note apologizing for you behavior last evening. Your upset was unexpected. In my experience every young lady looks forward to making her come-out with much excitement. It didn't occur to me you would feel otherwise."

Amilie held her tea saucer and cup steady with both hands as she lowered them to her lap. "I have never known anyone who made a come-out in London. The local squire's father presented his daughter at a ball in our assembly rooms. People still speak of the grand affair, but I was too young to attend." She looked at Lady Brompton and spoke directly. "I fear I would be a disappointment to you and Lord Brompton."

"The choice to have a come-out or to go to London at all is yours to make Amilie. I do not demand that you accede to my wishes in this matter."

Amilie looked down at the teacup she was holding in her lap. "I thank you for your understanding, and I am glad I accepted your invitation to have this visit."

Amilie sat for some time staring into her lap. By the time she looked up, Lady Brompton was halfway to the doors of the drawing room.

Amilie pushed herself up and out of the chair in her sitting room. She winced and groaned as a sharp pain streaked across the small of her back.

Checking the hour she was surprised to find she had

been sitting for more than half an hour, caught up in working the blank canvas Helaine found and brought to her. As usual, plying a needle erased the awareness of anything else.

Placing her hands over her hips, she hobbled to the bell chord on the wall of her sitting room to summon Helaine then managed to ease into the chair again and arrange herself into a semi-comfortable position.

"Miss? Is it tea you are wanting?" Helaine asked poking her head around the half-opened door.

"No, I need to tell you, I cannot make the trip to the village today."

"What is wrong, miss? Are you sick? Did her ladyship forbid you from going?" Genuine concern sounded in Helaine's voice.

Amilie gave a negative shake of her head. "I sent a note asking her permission, and she has given it. And I am not sick, exactly."

Helaine entered the room, closing the door behind her. Amilie saw the worry in Helaine's eyes.

"Then what is it, miss?"

"My hip and back muscles are stiff and complain each time I move. Walking a long distance today is not possible."

Helaine smiled and relaxed her shoulders. "It's the riding, miss. Mr. Fitzhugh will be disappointed if you do not join him. His enjoyment of his cakes will be spoiled."

"I shall write a note to inform him not to expect me."

"You could request a carriage, miss."

Amilie sighed. "Being driven such a short distance seems a frivolous luxury to me. However, since I am eager to purchase some dress fabric and complete my other errands I shall this once. How does one request a carriage?"

"I will notify the stables. One o'clock, miss?"

"One o'clock is fine. That should give me enough time to finish everything I wish to do and get to the confectioner's by two o'clock."

"What do you wish brought for your lunch?"

"A pot of tea, some buttered bread, and marmalade. I do not want to ruin my appetite for cakes."

"Yes, miss."

"And Helaine, after you request the carriage and bring my lunch, you are free until it is time for us to leave. My demands on you these past days have given you little time to yourself."

"Thank you, miss." Helaine hurried off in a rush and failed to close the hall door all the way.

Amilie attempted to stand and groaned. She forced herself to her feet and hobbled to the door, pushing it shut, then continued around the room hoping to ease the tightness across her hips.

After several lumbering trips around her sitting room, she surrendered to the pain, picked up her book, and eased into a chair to read.

When Helaine returned with the tray, Amilie inquired about obtaining bath water. "A long soak in hot water might help ease the tightness in my hips."

"Cook has tonight's dinner well underway. A beef

roast is rotating on the spit and the oyster pies are ready to bake. I will ask if there is room to heat water for you so it will be ready when we return."

"And the arrangements for the carriage?"

"The carriage will be in the courtyard at one o'clock."

"Then meet me in the entrance hall at the correct hour. No need for you to make a trip up the stairs."

"Yes, miss. You can manage the stairs alone in your condition?"

"If I give myself enough time, I believe I can."

Amilie ate a bit of bread and marmalade then sipped warm tea and gazed into the cold fireplace. A vision of Fitzhugh's face coiled into her mind. *Why is he being so kind to me? Is he bored here and finds me an amusing dalliance to wile away the hours before he returns to the pleasures of town? Perhaps he finds me naïve and defenseless against his charm, unable to flap strong wings and nip like the gander.*

"Does it matter?" Amilie asked aloud, forcing herself to her feet. "He will be gone soon. The end of the month he said. And as much as I am enjoying my time here, I may be gone sooner than he."

Determined to ignore her pain, she strode to the writing desk, and finished the letter to her friend. Then she began a note to the vicar who replaced her father. It was proper to welcome the vicar and his family to their new home and parish, the home and the parish she loved so dearly and missed so thoroughly. Sorrow flooded into her heart, roiled her stomach, and collided with the pain in her hips.

"Stop." Amilie heard the word echo through her sitting room. But this time it was not Mr. Fitzhugh shouting, the sound came from deep within her. It sounded like the shout her father made when she was three years old and had got too close to the road. Amilie covered her face with her hands.

"Your fortunes are great, look around you." Amilie could hear her father's voice speak the words he used so often at the beginning of his sermons.

Keeping her face in her hands and her eyes closed, the song her mother sang to her each night before kissing her cheek and tucking the bedcovers tight around her ran through her mind. She began to hum the tune of "Watt's Cradle Song," then added the words. "Sleep my babe; thy food and raiment, house and home thy friends provide . . . all thy wants are well supplied."

When Amilie came to the end of the second verse, a peaceful feeling smoothed out her ragged emotions. She could go on. She could find the strength to face the future.

Handed up by a footman, Amilie stepped into the well-appointed carriage. Her hips and legs protested each step of the way, but the steady determination of her spirit, the promise of new dress fabric, treats at the confectioner's shop and . . . and, the pleasure of being in Mr. Fitzhugh's company persuaded her to continue.

Helaine clambered into the carriage, pulling herself

up, and sat opposite Amilie. The carriage started forward. As it sped down the lane to the road, rounded the open gates, and headed in the direction of the village, Amilie gripped the edge of the upholstered seat. The carriage was going so fast, when she looked out the window, the landscape was a blur. Fearing she would find herself on the carriage floor if they hit a rut, Amilie tightened her grip to the edge of the seat.

When the carriage stopped in front of the mercer's shop, she caught her breath and reflected aloud on her carriage ride.

"One fails to enjoy a great deal when enclosed by the walls of a carriage. The small sounds made by the wind, the voices of the animals, the perfume of the flowers, seasonal changes in the landscape."

"'Tis true, miss. But a carriage lessens the time it takes to get where you are going. Errands or visiting, either one."

Amilie sighed. "I suppose. My schedule has never been so filled I found it necessary to scurry from place to place."

The footman stepped down from his station at the rear of the carriage, pulled open the door, unfolded the steps, and offered a gloved hand to assist Amilie's descent.

She lowered her right foot to the step and clamped her bottom lip under her teeth as a sharp pain darted across her mid-section. She stood still and breathed in measured breaths as she waited for Helaine to emerge from the carriage and give instructions to the driver.

She got into the mercer's shop without Helaine's assistance. The interior of the shop was hushed and expectant, dust motes danced along a beam of sunlight that intruded into the dim reaches of the shop. The proprietor emerged from the back room wiping his hands on a cloth, his beaming face expressing his delight.

"Welcome, Miss Jasperton. Your patronage of my humble shop again today is a high honor." His head bobbed a toothy smile like a ship's lantern in a storm.

"I wish to purchase fabric sufficient for a dress. Perhaps from the bolt you displayed yesterday if the price is not too dear."

"Your new bonnet trim looks most fetching, Miss Jasperton. Your eye for fashion and a good bargain is keen. Extremely so."

The mercer reached under the counter and lifted a bolt of gray cloth to the top of the counter. "You are the first of my customers to view this bolt of the finest woolcloth. It would make up into a fine, warm pelisse to wear when the weather cools.

"It is kind of you to anticipate my needs, Mr. White. However, today my interest is in purchasing dress fabric."

"Of course," the proprietor clapped his hands together. Within seconds, a young man emerged through the curtain covering the doorway that gave entrance to the back room.

The proprietor gave the young man instructions and the bolt of pale pink silk Amilie admired the day before was placed on the counter for her to examine. When an acceptable charge per yard was given, Amilie placed her order.

The young assistant took the bolt to the cutting table while the mercer draped a section of the woolcloth for Amilie's closer inspection.

"This is a quality wool, soft but tightly woven, highly suitable for a pelisse," the mercer said.

The length of silk is all for today," Amilie said as she fingered the fine wool.

The assistant returned, wrapped the length of silk with care and tied the package securely. Amilie opened her reticule, took out her purse, and counted out the coins.

The proprietor backed away, disbelief radiating from his face. "I am prepared to extend credit, Miss Jasperton. The cost of your purchases can be settled the same as Brompton Manor's."

Amilie pulled herself up as far as she could and winced at the pain the exertion caused. She pursed her lips. "I thank you, sir, but I am paying for my purchases at the time I make them. I do not wish them added to Brompton Manor's account.

The proprietor looked at Helaine who was standing behind and to one side of Amilie, gave a quick nod of his head, and returned his attention to Amilie.

"Of course, Miss Jasperton," the mercer said as he picked up the coins. You are most wise for such a young woman. "It is a pleasure to have your patronage." The proprietor grumbled words that were unclear as he came around the counter to escort her to the door of the shop. Amilie handed the package with her purchase to Helaine and complimented the mercer on his fine shop.

When they reached the footpath boarding the road

outside the mercer's shop, Amilie sighed. "I confess, Helaine, the woolcloth tempted me sorely. It was good the proprietor terminated his attempt to persuade me before I weakened."

"If I may be bold, miss?"

"Say what you wish, Helaine?"

"The proprietor, Mr. White, had his shop in London for many years and often recounts stories of how he could persuade even the most sophisticated of town shoppers to buy extra goods. You did well to resist his practiced attempt to sell you the woolcloth. Lovely as it was."

Amilie turned to look at Helaine and noted a spark of mischief in Helaine's eyes which disappeared in a blink.

"May I make a request?" Helaine asked.

"Of course."

"If you approve, I should like to return to the mercer's shop after you join Mr. Fitzhugh. My cousin is wife to his son. A visit with her would be nice."

"Of course, you may have a visit with your cousin. I have decided to postpone a stop at the subscription library until a time when my back is not so pained. Once the carriage is in front of the confectioner's, I shall go to the stationery shop next door to make my purchase then return to the carriage to await Mr. Fitzhugh. As soon as he arrives, you may be off."

In the stationery shop, Amilie bought writing paper and a new blotter. Back in the carriage, she and Helaine spoke about their needlework projects. At five minutes past two o'clock, according to Amilie's timepiece, she leaned her head out the window. Mr. Fitzhugh was a block away coming toward the confectioner's shop at a near run.

She waved to him.

Standing at the side of the carriage door, breathing hard, Fitzhugh looked up at Amilie. "I am in shock, Miss Jasperton."

"You are quite out of breath, Mr. Fitzhugh."

"The tailor took longer than expected. I worried you would think I had forgotten."

"I arrived early, due to my use of this wheeled conveyance and a pair of sprightly horses."

"Shocking, Miss Jasperton, seeing you in a carriage. I hope my influence on you about speeding up has not overtaken your preference for walking."

"I shall explain my use of a carriage today in a moment, Mr. Fitzhugh. Helaine is returning to the mercer's shop for a visit with her cousin. I think a return here in . . . ?"

"Thirty minutes, miss?"

"Thirty minutes."

Amilie accepted Fitzhugh's hand as she stepped down from the carriage. Her shoe caught the hem of her dress. She pitched forward and found herself entangled in Mr. Fitzhugh arms. His arms tightened about her, crushing her to his chest.

"Miss, Are you hurt?" Helaine asked peering through the carriage door opening.

Fitzhugh sat Amilie on her feet and took a step back. His breathing more labored than before.

Amilie reached up and straightened the brim of her bonnet then patted her dress skirt, all the while desperately trying to breathe. Opening her mouth wide and taking in a large quantity of air, she forced herself to speak.

"I am fine, Helaine. My sincere apology for falling on you, Mr. Fitzhugh. I hope my fall has not caused you to suffer scrapes and bruises."

The grin splitting Fitzhugh's face and the wicked gleam in his eyes disconcerted her. Surely, he thought her clumsy—incapable of descending gracefully from a carriage because of her unfamiliarity with riding in one.

"Off to your visit," Amilie said waving the back of her hand to Helaine and feeling the heat of embarrassment in her cheeks.

"Enjoy your treat, miss."

Amilie returned her attention to Fitzhugh and caught him giving a wink to Helaine. This time there was no question in her mind. He had winked. Was this a signal arranged by them when they were children, an innocent flirtation between a man and a woman who had known each other since childhood or a serious affair between two adults?

"You are limping, Miss Jasperton," he said as he held the door of the confectioner's shop. "Did you injure yourself after all?"

"My limp explains my use of the carriage and my clumsy descent. My riding lessons are a pleasure, but my muscles are protesting."

"Sitting in a saddle can be taxing. I have often suffered in the same way."

Laughing, Amilie and Fitzhugh entered the confectioner's establishment. It was the sweetest smelling shop Amilie had ever been inside.

Easing down into one of the chairs that ringed a small table, Amilie took the paper menu and read aloud the listing of the day's offerings. "What are ices, Mr. Fitzhugh?" she asked after coming to the section listing the flavor of ices available.

Fitzhugh blinked at her as his head popped up from his own perusal of the menu. "You are not familiar with ices?"

"I fear not."

"Then you shall discover ices today and be tempted ever after."

The proprietor came from around a display case to stand next to their table.

"A pineapple ice and your best tea for Miss Jasperton, and a plate of your small cakes and the same tea for me."

"It has been some time, Mr. Fitzhugh, since you stopped in to enjoy my cakes. Happy to have you back, sir."

Fitzhugh nodded at the proprietor who swung around and headed back toward the display case.

Amilie marveled when the frozen treat was set before her.

"Take a taste Miss Jasperton; the flavorful concoction begins to melt if you linger."

Amilie raised a spoonful to her mouth. "This is so cold and so delicious. How is it possible to make an ice in this temperate weather, Mr. Fitzhugh?"

"The ice is collected and stored in icehouses. Brompton Manor has its own icehouse. Perhaps we might make a tour one day. I think you would find it of interest."

"Helaine mentioned there was an icehouse on the grounds, constructed the same time as the orangery."

"Try one of my cakes, Miss Jasperton. They are truly as delicious as my memory declared them."

"Half of a cake is fine. I understand Cook has a large roast of beef on the spit and there will be an oyster pie on the table tonight."

"A most substantial dinner awaits us then. All the same, since I am benefiting from the exercise of being afoot, I shall enjoy my cakes without regard."

"You came to the village on foot today?"

"In the mistaken belief, I have since learned, I would have the opportunity to enjoy your company on the return."

"You are welcome to join us in the carriage."

"Thank you for your kind offer, but I shall choose to go home as I came away. You have inspired me to slow my pace, and, to my surprise, I have found a slower pace to my liking."

"But I see you forget at times and resume your former speed."

"You are most observant, Miss Jasperton."

The proprietor set the fragrant tea on the table. They each concentrated on their treats.

Amilie swallowed the last of her ice. "Tell me of your time in America. What did you find of interest in our former colonies?"

Fitzhugh stared at the wall above Amilie's head and cleared his throat. "I found myself in the most exotic locale—a place called New Orleans."

"But Orleans is in France, is it not?"

"The French established New Orleans on the North American continent. Both France and Spain held claim to the ground at various times. And then Napoleon sold it to the Americans. The area in which I found myself retains the flavor of the French and Spanish influence. It is not at all like the original British colonies."

"You were involved in trading there?"

The fork carrying a piece of cake to Fitzhugh's mouth hung suspended halfway between the plate and his lips. Then he laid the fork down on the plate and looked at Amilie with eyes clouded with pain. "My journey to New Orleans was ordered by the king. I was a captain in the regiment that fought unsuccessfully against the Americans at the battle of New Orleans."

"I see," Amilie said. Her voice subdued. "Perhaps America is not a fit subject at the moment."

Fitzhugh coughed, picked up the fork that still held the bite of cake, and inserted it into his mouth. He chewed for several seconds and swallowed.

"Some of my memories of America are not so pleasant, Miss Jasperton. Tell me about your father's work? I resigned my commission on my return and am considering the church."

"The work of the church suited my father, a stern but merciful and humorous gentleman. I think those are necessary traits to possess if one is to assume a responsibility for people's souls."

"Then church and I should suit well. Helaine has provided me a fine example of how to be stern, the Army has taught me how to be merciful, and Lord Brompton has taught me humor."

"I wish you the best in your endeavor."

"And what visions do you hold for your future, Miss Jasperton?"

Amilie glanced out the window of the confectioner's shop. Helaine and the carriage were standing at the curb.

"Goodness thirty minutes has flown by. The carriage is returned and waiting. I offer you a seat again, Mr. Fitzhugh, in case you should reconsider."

"Thank you, but a slower pace appeals at the moment."

"Enjoy your return then. I am in envy of you. So much beauty is missed when traveling by carriage."

"And speed leaves one with little time to ponder the proper course one should take to meet the challenges before them," Fitzhugh said.

Chapter Eight

As Amilie and Fitzhugh were enjoying their treat, the countess of Brompton was visiting the dower house and was seated in a chair next to the earl of Brompton's bed.

Propped up in the bed by three plumped pillows supporting his back, the earl of Brompton, his bald pate hidden beneath a wool nightcap and his once-broad shoulders draped with a fur-trimmed, cashmere shawl, looked cheerful. His face was ruddy. The ashy undertone of the past few weeks replaced with a healthy glow.

"I declare our granddaughter will make a fine wife for my cousin's son, George. And when the Brompton title passes to my cousin, Mullerton, George's father, then George will be the next in line for the Brompton title and Amilie, as his wife, will one day hold your honorary rank of countess and take your place in society."

He turned to look at the woman who had become his countess and waggled his eyebrows. "Of course, no one will ever be able to match you my dearest, but Amilie will do a splendid job." The earl of Brompton settled back into the pillows and beamed.

"My dear Brompton . . . ," Lady Brompton began.

The earl of Brompton continued on as though she had not spoken. "When Amilie marries George my responsibility to see someone carrying my sensible and practical traits in a position to influence the titleholder will be discharged."

"But, Brompton . . ."

"Given that both my cousin, who stands to inherit, and his son George are beef-witted, George especially so, I feel pressed to see this accomplished. Amilie exhibits the best of my characteristics. She is adventuresome, resilient, and frugal. George will be well-served to have her as his countess."

Lady Brompton placed the netting she was working aside and reached over to place her hand atop the hands of her beloved husband. "Brompton, our influence on this outcome is limited. The invitation to your cousin and his family has been sent. They are expected to arrive day after tomorrow. If the two young people take a liking to one another, we shall celebrate. Otherwise, we are not to force Amilie to accept a marriage she does not desire. I will not lose her too."

The earl of Brompton sputtered. His face grew ruddier. "My dear, I do not understand what prevents a marriage arrangement from being ordered. The young ladies flock around gentlemen in line to inherit titles and prosperous estates. They do everything that is proper to attract an offer from one of these fortunate gentlemen."

"Like her mother, Amilie's ideas may be different."

"I say. No one allowed us the freedom to make an impractical and unwise choice of mates. I did mention to my father, on several occasions, I favored you . . . ," the earl added with a sly smile, ". . . he let me fret for weeks before speaking with your father."

"Perhaps there is an inherited stubbornness that passes through the female line. Your daughter certainly, and I sense Amilie possesses a will as strong as her mother's."

"I never forgave our daughter for defying us by refusing to marry my cousin. Mullerton is beef-witted, but she was born to a position of privilege and held a responsibility to the title. Her refusal to honor her place broke my heart. I quake in my boots when I think of my cousin taking the title with his cork-brained wife as countess. I mean to stay alive as long as possible."

"Brompton, Matilda Mullerton is not cork-brained."

"Well she married my cousin didn't she?"

"Brompton!" Lady Brompton sat back in her chair. "You know I am in agreement with you about duty and responsibility, but perhaps our wish is not to prevail this time either. We have been given this chance to enjoy our granddaughter. She is a delightful young woman. I have no intention of sending her away."

The earl of Brompton swiped at his cheeks with the

hem of the bed sheet. "Our granddaughter is a beautiful young woman, as beautiful as her mother, and in possession of my natural charm. Once you have smoothed off any rough edges she acquired from living in such poor circumstances, I imagine she will be the belle of the upcoming season. And George's desire for her is guaranteed, or I do not know the ways of a young gentleman."

"She may not wish to participate in the events of the season, Brompton. The mere mention of a come-out seemed to frighten her."

"Pshaw. Since she has my fortitude, she cannot be frightened at the prospect of enjoying a season."

"Making a come-out is a rigorous undertaking for a young lady. All eyes are on her when she is in public, and the gossip's tongues await her slightest misstep. Refrain from mentioning anything about this in her presence. The subject requires a delicate approach."

"You are right, my dear, as always." The earl of Brompton's lips turned down and his lower lip poked out.

"And Brompton, before I forget, I suspect Amilie and Fitzhugh are developing a *tendre* for one another."

At this news, the earl of Brompton bolted upright and gave in to a fit of coughing. Lady Brompton jumped to her feet, pounding on his back until he recovered.

"Brompton, I am calling for the physician!"

"No need for the physician. Your remark caught me by surprise. Did you know Fitzhugh has resigned his commission and is considering the church?"

Lady Brompton sat down. Then she began to laugh

so hard tears streamed down her cheeks. The earl of Brompton could not contain his own laughter, clutched his stomach, and called for mercy.

"I have not the breath to laugh so lustily," he gasped.

Gaining control, Lady Brompton stood up, took the earl of Brompton's hand, and kissed his cheek.

"Perhaps the sensible and practical traits you passed to your progeny are the traits that drew your daughter to a man of the church and perhaps they are the traits that lead your granddaughter in the same direction."

"But I never considered the church."

"Brompton, what a silly thing to say. As the first born son of an earl, your future was determined the day you were born."

"My uncle never considered the church."

"And sired a beef-witted son."

Once again, the earl of Brompton and Lady Brompton broke into raucous laughter.

"Come Sunday, I shall be in my pew for services— the first time in many months."

"Imagine the delight on the rector's face when he sees you in your usual place, nodding your agreement to his somber pronouncements."

"If born a second son, I would have chosen the church. My lengthy suffering forced me to spend hours contemplating the afterlife. I rather enjoyed myself."

"The afterlife can wait. Thoughts of the opening of Parliament are in order."

"I look forward to hearing the Reverend Littleton's

earnest exhortations once again." The earl of Brompton smiled at his beloved mate then reached over and affectionately pinched her cheek. "Reinforcing one's moral strength is always good before tackling the business of the nation."

Lady Brompton bent down to kiss the earl of Brompton's forehead. "Cook is preparing many of your favorite dishes for dinner this evening."

"Then I shall have a short nap before dressing. Tell Willers to wake me in an hour and bring along my portable writing desk when he comes."

Outside the dower house, Lady Brompton sniffed the sweetly scented air. "You may return to the stables," she said to the gig driver. "I will walk back to the Manor house."

Turning into the carriage lane that wound upward to the Manor house, a loud voice hailed her. She halted in the middle of the path and turned to see who had called to her.

Fitzhugh, with his long legs in full stride was gaining on her.

"How odd to see you afoot, Fitzhugh," she said merrily as he caught up to her.

"Perhaps I am learning the value of slowing down."

"Miss Jasperton is a good influence on you, then."

"Your granddaughter is an intelligent and charming young lady. I find her refreshing after having spent such a long time in the company of armed men."

Lady Brompton turned to observe Fitzhugh's face. "Are you developing tender feelings for Amilie, Fitzhugh?"

"Your ladyship, I think . . . I . . . I do not know the answer to your question." Looking away Fitzhugh began talking of the fine weather they were enjoying then remarked on the changes made on the estate while he was away.

Lady Brompton placed her hand on Fitzhugh's sleeve to stop his senseless chatter and get his full attention.

"Fitzhugh, I have seen the look in your eye when you are observing Amilie. I caution you about encouraging her affections or letting your own overtake your senses. Amilie has lived a sheltered life, far different from the worldly society you are familiar with. She has neither the protection of sophistication nor the studied coyness possessed by the other young ladies of your acquaintance."

"I thank you for the warning, your ladyship. It is not my desire to have Miss Jasperton mistake my friendship for more."

They continued on toward the Manor house, their conversation limited to remarking on the flowers lining the path.

In the entrance hall, Lady Brompton untied the ribbons of her bonnet and pulled off her gloves. Fitzhugh handed his hat and gloves to the footman on duty.

"Fitzhugh, join me in the conservatory." Her eyes compelled him not to make an excuse.

Once seated in the sunny, plant filled room, she continued her earlier conversation.

"The Mullertons are to arrive here the day after to-morrow. You remember George, of course?"

"I remember George only too well."

"I expect you to behave civilly toward the Mullertons and especially toward George. I am sure he is a more pleasant person now that he has matured."

"London." Fitzhugh jumped to his feet and moved a short distance up the flagstone path of the conservatory. "I shall leave for London at dawn."

"You will remain here, Fitzhugh and face the inevitable. Brompton waited a long time for your return. With no word of your whereabouts for so long, my dear Brompton worried so. He hounded the Army daily, but they provided no answer. I believe having you back and in good health has speeded his recovery. He expects you to stay the length of time you stated in your letter you would be here."

Lady Brompton shifted her position on the bench as Fitzhugh rejoined her. She lowered her voice as though speaking only to herself. "He has expressed many times his wish you were his heir. But, we are bound by law and the passing of the title and the entailed estates is determined by law. The law disregards one's heart."

Fitzhugh managed a wan smile. "I find I have a great deal in common with Miss Jasperton. She is separated from everything she knew and loved, and I face the same fate."

Lady Brompton reached across to place her hand atop his. "Does she confide in you?"

"Not in words, but I often see her sadness deep within her eyes."

"Perhaps she and George will suit. And George can make her happy again."

"You intend Amilie to accept George in marriage? You would see her wed to a gentleman of low character, cowardice, and despicable habits?"

Lady Brompton rose to her feet. Fitzhugh rose with her.

Lady Brompton's face masked the authority her position afforded her. "I know you do not think highly of George, but he is in line for the Brompton title. Our desire is for George and Amilie to become acquainted with one another. That is all."

Fitzhugh pivoted to face the conservatory doors. The sound made by the soles of his boots hitting the flagstones as he walked off expressed his anger without words.

Lady Brompton bowed her head for a few seconds. Then, with her chin up, she strolled along the serpentine paths, examining the plants, pinching off a spent flower or a brown leaf, and listening to the songs of the caged birds.

Chapter Nine

After returning from the village, Amilie climbed the stairs to her apartments and lay down on her counterpane as she waited for Helaine to return with a tub and hot bath water for a soak to ease the soreness in her muscles. The pain in her back and legs had been forgotten in Fitzhugh's company, but once she attempted the stairs it returned sharper than before.

Hearing Helaine in the sitting room directing a footman to place the tub in front of the sitting room fire, she lay still until Helaine poked her head around the doorframe.

"Miss?"

"Your return is sooner than I expected, Helaine."

"Yes, miss. Cook put the bath water on to heat before we left for the village. I promised her I would help with the Christmas puddings."

Amilie laughed. "So, to see to my pain, you have burdened yourself with added duties."

Helaine bowed her head and clasped her hands together in front of her apron. "Helping with the Christmas puddings is really not so much a burden, miss. Every year, before me mum passed, I prepared a big Christmas pudding with her for the staff to have at their Christmas meal. Helping the new cook reminds me of those times I helped me mum."

"To think of the approaching Christmas holiday without my parents is the worst pain," Amilie said, dropping her head and turning away.

"It is, miss." Helaine lifted her head and bustled about, poking the coals in the grate, placing towels on a stand, and pouring the hot water into the tin tub. She squeezed a few drops of rose oil into the bath water. "Come, miss, while the water is hot."

Amilie got into the tub and managed to sit, sounding only a low groan. She closed her eyes and settled against the high-sloped back of the tub. The hot water was soothing.

Helaine added fresh coals to the grate. "A heated brick to warm your sheets tonight and some camphor liniment to rub on your back might give relief, miss. When her ladyship's fingers ache, she uses my liniment. It could help with your back."

"The promise of warm sheets and a liniment rub at the end of the evening is welcome. Thinking of sitting at the table through a long dinner and trying to rise afterward was troubling me. I considered asking to borrow a walking stick from Lord Brompton or making my excuses and having my dinner in my sitting room. But with a liniment rub to look forward to, I shall go forward and dine at table."

Helaine stood next to the tub with a shift in her hands. "Your wardrobe is in disarray, miss. I will straighten things and lay out your clothing for tonight while you finish your bath.

When Helaine disappeared through the bedchamber door, Amilie placed her hands on the edge of the tub and pushed herself to her feet. She toweled dry, then slipped the clean, dry shift over her head.

When Amilie entered the drawing room, Lord and Lady Brompton were already seated in chairs drawn up close to the fire.

"Do sit here, beside me," Lady Brompton said patting the seat next to hers. "Fitzhugh sent word his cravat is refusing to cooperate this evening and his appearance will be delayed.

Amilie dipped a small curtsy, making only a tiny grimace, as she sat down in the chair. "Mr. Fitzhugh manages very impressive cravats," she said and laughed. "It is curious to see how he has chosen to twist the length of white cloth around his neck each day."

"Vanity, I fear," sputtered the earl of Brompton.

"Fitzhugh is not being vain, Brompton. When he passed through London on his way home, he found his friends dressing with a new, somewhat complicated simplicity. He is trying to emulate them so his dress will match theirs when he returns to Town. He has placed a large order at the village tailor shop."

"Fitzhugh is a handsome devil. Always been favored and spoiled by the ladies. Once he is in circulation again, the state of his cravat is bound to suffer from rouge and powder. Before he leaves, I intend to counsel him against traps and plots devised by the ladies awaiting his return to London."

Amilie's smile deserted her face. The charming gentleman, who had helped ease her sorrow and offered her his friendship, had his choice of beautiful and accomplished, society ladies. Somehow, before his charms overtook her sensibilities, she needed to repair the wall around her heart he had begun to dismantle.

"Ahoy, me mates," Fitzhugh boomed, making his way across the room in their direction.

"Such crude language, Fitzhugh. Those expressions are proper only when you are with friends, not when you are in the company of a proper young lady." Lady Brompton raised her quizzing glass to her eye and leaned closer to Fitzhugh.

Fitzhugh bowed. A grin split his face. "You are right, your ladyship. My manners are abominable. My sincere apology to Miss Jasperton." Fitzhugh winked his eye, nodded at Amilie, and dropped into a chair.

"My lord, my lady, Miss Jasperton, it is my pleasure to join you after some difficulty. I offer sincere apologies for my late arrival and the delay of your dinner."

The assembled party laughed, with varying degrees

of merriment. The earl of Brompton's guffaw's sounded more like snorts.

"Your cravat is very creative. Lopsided and quite wrinkled," the earl of Brompton said looking toward Fitzhugh and giving him a sly grin.

"I gave up trying to tie the wretched thing into a decent tie. The expression on my valet's face grew darker each time I discarded a length of starched cloth. I thought to end it all at last and give him relief." Fitzhugh stood and offered his arm to Amilie.

"The simplest tie is often the most elegant, Fitzhugh," Lady Brompton said.

"My lady, since I find I am a fumble finger, I count on your assessment. I intend to keep to only rudimentary arrangements for my cravats from now on."

"Your behavior tonight is very strange, Fitzhugh. You didn't contract an exotic disease while in America did you?" the earl of Bromton asked.

"I contracted something after learning George Mullerton is expected."

Amilie's confusion over this conversation increased. *Who was George Mullerton? And why was Fitzhugh so upset by the upcoming visit of this person he could not manage to tie his cravat?*

"Dinner has waited long enough. The staff shall be in a tizzy. Let us tarry here no longer."

Amilie noted the look Lady Brompton gave Fitzhugh. There was fire in Lady Brompton's eyes.

The party proceeded in the same order as they had

on previous evenings—the earl of Brompton in the lead assisted by a footman, Amilie on one of Fitzhugh's arms, and Lady Brompton on the other.

The dinner table did not disappoint.

Amilie helped herself from many of the dishes that ringed her place setting. Her appetite had returned. She did not raise her eyes from her plate from fear of seeing Fitzhugh across from her and losing her appetite again.

After swallowing a bite of poached turbot, Lady Brompton gave her attention to Amilie. "You ordered a carriage to convey you to the village today."

Amilie wiped her lips and smiled. "I found myself incapable of walking any distance today. My muscles are not yet adjusted to the saddle and are in full protest."

The earl of Brompton's face perked up. "Glad you mentioned horses, my dear. I am certain to ride again soon. The thought of being atop Moonfire encourages me in my struggles to recover my strength." He spooned a large portion of the oyster pie onto his plate. "Fitzhugh, I am delighted you have returned in time to accompany me for my first ride. The groom is not to ride with me. He would spoil my pleasure. He scowls at me because he thinks I work Moonfire too hard, but I know my horse and Moonfire knows me far better than the groom does."

Fitzhugh laughed. "I think the groom's time is fully engaged attending Miss Jasperton during her riding lessons and overseeing the well-being of Shining Star."

Surprised, Amilie lifted her eyes from her plate and

looked across the table. Fitzhugh's sparkling eyes looked back, challenging her, disturbing her senses. She could not enjoy her dinner and look into his eyes. Looking into his eyes did something odd to her stomach. She struggled to break eye contact with him and think of a light-hearted response to his teasing.

"Shining Star expresses a great fondness for me. She is responsive to my commands. I should think the groom is pleased I am so little trouble."

Fitzhugh met her stare then looked away, swiveled his eyes downward and forked up a piece of roast duck. He shoved the roast fowl into his mouth, chewed and swallowed, while avoiding Amilie and speaking only to the earl of Brompton. "Tell us the grand story of your first stag hunt."

"I still have the trophy that was awarded me," the earl of Brompton said as he began the gruesome and grueling tale of his passage into manhood.

"Brompton. That is enough. The reward you received for killing your first stag is not fit for Amilie's ears. Enjoy your dinner while you listen to Amilie recount her visit to the village today. If any of the platters are returned untouched, you will upset Cook and she will resign."

The glee vanished from the earl of Brompton's face, but he complied with Lady Brompton's instruction and scanned the table. Lady Brompton commented on several of the village shops. Amilie related her experience at the confectioner's and her delight over her first taste of an ice, but she made no mention of Fitzhugh being there with her.

The earl of Brompton gestured and grunted, sending footmen down the table to bring him the bowls and platters that were out of his reach. Fitzhugh twirled the stem of his glass, keeping his hands busy and his eyes away from Amilie.

"So, my child, you had an enjoyable outing today."

"I did, in spite of my sore muscles. Helaine's suggestion that I order a carriage enabled me to go ahead with the trip to the village.

"And did you purchase anything today?"

"I did. But the nature of my purchase, I hope to keep as a surprise."

Amilie glanced at Fitzhugh. Her heart quivered as she watched him concentrate on folding his serviette into a square.

She began to prattle. "It was a grand experience. I was quite breathless when the carriage pulled in front of the mercer's. Riding in such a fine carriage, pulled by the finest of horses was a delight. But I do think the slower pace of walking is better suited to my nature."

Lady Brompton spoke up, interrupting Amilie's soliloquy. "Your walking has set a good example for me, Amilie. When I came from the dower house today, I sent the gig driver off and proceeded on foot toward the Manor house. The fresh air was restorative. I watched the bees flitting about from flower to flower, so restful to the eyes, and then to my surprise Fitzhugh caught up with me on the path. It was a shock to see him on foot." Lady Brompton laughed with much glee and looked in Fitzhugh's direction. Then the tone of her voice changed to a more serious tenor. "Walking with Fitzhugh today gave us an opportunity for some needed conversation." She turned her eyes to the earl of Brompton. "I should have missed the pleasure had I returned to the Manor in the gig."

Amilie had no idea what to make of the conversation going on around her. There had to be unspoken messages beneath Lady Brompton's words tonight. The earl of Brompton looked pleased. Fitzhugh looked discomfited.

"Fitzhugh afoot?" the earl of Brompton boomed, turning away from the dish of rabbit stew and looking at his ward. "Did something happen to your horse? Is that the reason you appear undone tonight?"

"Nothing is wrong with my horse. Miss Jasperton has convinced me a person is capable of slowing down and propelling themselves forward without the aid of a horse."

Amilie arranged her utensils across her plate, dabbed at her lips, and forced her eyes to stay away from Fitzhugh's dark curls and penetrating eyes.

When Lady Brompton got to her feet, Amilie followed her lead.

"Brompton . . . ," Lady Brompton begain ". . . if you do not linger long at table tonight, I believe Amilie is prepared to perform for us this evening."

"In that case, I shall enlist Fitzhugh to watch the time. One-half hour gives me enough time to relate the story of my first stag hunt—in some detail."

* * *

The two gentlemen sat in silence as Lady Brompton and Amilie proceeded from the dining room. The butler set out a fine French brandy and fresh glasses, as the footmen removed the last of the dishes and utensils. The earl of Brompton pushed himself up to his feet and, with the aide of his walking stick, managed the short distance to the sideboard that concealed the chamber pot.

Returning to the table, he poured brandy into two glasses, lifted his glass to Fitzhugh, and offered a toast. "To our health and to our wealth." The earl of Brompton sniffed the amber liquid and swilled it around the bowl of the glass. "The French are talented at distilling grapes, but in all other things they are incompetents and petty tyrants. Napoleon reflects the nation. They have been defeated over and over again by superior British troops. Wellington is a military genius. We are fortunate he is on our side." The earl of Brompton took a sip of the brandy then set the glass aside. "It is a great sadness to me that we have been forced to direct so much of the Nation's effort and treasure to fend off our warring French neighbors. It has crippled our efforts to prevail against the Americans. Time and again, we find ourselves bested by our own relatives and friends. Have they become barbarians in their new land, Fitzhugh?"

"The Americans retain their British grit. I did not find they had become barbarians. One of their generals a man named Andrew Jackson, used our own military tactics to defeat us at the battle of New Orleans. I. . . ."

"What happened there by the way? The newspapers

were full of stories, but it was never clear to me what caused our defeat.

"It was a very unfortunate situation. We had no chance of prevailing." Fitzhugh took a long sip from his glass. "As I lay wounded, I watched a mass grave being dug and hundreds of my fellow soldiers buried in foreign soil."

"And you were captured and held prisoner by the American forces?"

"Not captured, wounded. Early in the battle, a bullet pierced the calf of my right leg, and I fell behind the advancing line. Unable to go forward, I lay on the ground, partially concealed by a hedgerow, while the battle raged on. When dark descended and the sounds of battle stilled, a young lad who came to scavenge the battlefield, discovered me. He half-carried me to his cart and managed to heft me onto the cart bed."

"And he chose not to deliver you to his countrymen?"

"He took me to a private home and drove the cart through a gate in a wall into a rear courtyard. He then called for someone to assist him. They carried me inside and laid me in a bed. Sometime later, a surgeon, reeking of drink and sweat, came in to examine my wounds. In spite of his sorry condition, the surgeon treated me with skill. After my fever broke and my wounds started to heal, I gained my strength rapidly."

"And what did the people who saved you say to you?"

"They spoke in a dialect incomprehensible to me. I learned later the lad who rescued me, and the doctor who treated me, were of French and Spanish ancestry, the same as many of the people in the area who call themselves Creoles. Meaning native born, I later learned."

"And they treated you well?"

"Yes. I was fortunate. The lad who found me served a family who held a grievance against the Americans."

"Yes, well that is understandable."

"I was tended by a light-skinned African woman. Once my fever broke, she fed me a porridge made from soft-boiled rice, with milk stirred in. A spoonful at a time, until the day I ate the entire contents of the bowl and requested more. After that, she brought real food. Delicious, spicy food full of vegetables and meat."

The earl of Brompton blew his nose. "I shall be forever grateful to that fine family, Fitzhugh. We worried we would never see you again. When your letter from America arrived, it provided us great relief." The earl of Brompton wiped his eyes and nose then changed the subject. "Have you made your decision over what you wish to do in the future?"

"No. I am still considering the church."

The earl of Brompton looked across the rim of his raised glass and lowered it until the bottom of the glass hit the table. "I thought perhaps some land of your own would be your choice. I have land and a small manor house that are not covered by entail. A bit neglected, but with your good management, it could provide you a decent living if that is your wish."

"Your lordship, your offer is generous. Perhaps we can discuss my future at another time, when I am more settled and my mind is not so rattled. At the moment, the numbers on the clock indicate the ladies are expecting us."

While the gentleman enjoyed their time alone in the dining room, Amilie and Lady Brompton sat across from one another in the drawing room in chairs on either side of a tea table. After taking a sip of tea, Lady Brompton began to inform Amilie of the upcoming visit of the Mullertons.

"Our guests are to arrive day after tomorrow. Mr. Charles Mullerton, is a distant cousin of Brompton's and the heir presumptive to the Brompton title, his wife and their son George will be accompanying him.

"I look forward to meeting them." Amilie now understood Fitzhugh's reference about contending with George, but not why George's upcoming visit upset him. Amilie stared into her teacup for several seconds, then, putting a smile on her face, informed Lady Brompton about making a selection of two of Mozart's sonatas to perform for the earl of Brompton this evening.

"You were thoughtful to remember. Your grandfather finds great joy in music and to hear the music of Mozart being performed by his granddaughter will delight him."

"Lord Brompton looks well tonight."

"Brompton's color is much better and his appetite is returning. I believe he is on the way to a full restoration of his health." Her smile was sweet, her eyes reflecting her deep affection. But then she leaned forward, increasing the intimacy between herself and Amilie. Her eyes were watchful.

Amilie sensed some tension between them.

"It is pleasant to see you and Fitzhugh enjoying one another's company. You are close enough in age to share a friendship."

"Mr. Fitzhugh has been kind," Amilie said, hurrying her words in response to the quickening in her pulse at hearing Lady Brompton state such a thing. "Today, upon learning of my unfamiliarity with ices, he insisted I try a frozen treat and ordered the best quality tea and a pineapple ice for me," she blurted out.

Lady Brompton sat back in her chair. "So Fitzhugh joined you at the confectioner's today?" All traces of a lighthearted jest were missing. "I imagine he ordered a plate of cakes for himself."

"And generously offered one to me to sample."

"And licked frosting from his fingers at the same time?"

Amilie broke into giggles. "The chagrin on his face, when he saw me watching, reminded me of a lad caught playing with a toy during church service."

Lady Brompton's expression softened, her laugh mingled with Amilie's expressed merriment. "I am sorry Amilie. Fitzhugh has grown from a beautiful and enchanting lad into a handsome and charming gentleman. A delight to all of the young ladies he meets. Do not be blinded by his charm."

Amilie bit her bottom lip, breathed in deep, and

faced Lady Brompton. "I should like to speak to you at some length. I have many questions about many things."

"I am sure you do. We shall have a talk soon."

Chapter Ten

The earl of Brompton, assisted by Fitzhugh, shuffled into the drawing room. The two gentlemen took seats near Amilie and Lady Brompton.

"Amilie has offered to play for us this evening, Brompton."

"Delighted, my dear, delighted."

Amilie crossed the room to the mahogany pianoforte, softly tested the keys then began to play the Mozart pieces she practiced earlier.

Coming to the end of the second piece, she rose to her feet and dipped a curtsy. She nodded to Mr. Fitzhugh who had moved to stand beside the pianoforte.

"A skilled performance, Miss Jasperton, perhaps a stroll about the room is in order. I should be delighted to have the opportunity to introduce you to your hanging ancestors."

"Watch your words, Fitzhugh," the earl of Brompton said followed by a gleeful chortle. "Be skeptical of his stories, my dear child. Only one of those gentlemen was sent to the gallows. Found guilty of treason on the flimsiest of evidence. But he was hanged in public, in front of a jeering crowd, nonetheless."

Fitzhugh laughed. "Miss Jasperton is to guess which of her ancestor's ended up in such dire straits because of his vainglory. But I caution you ahead of time it is not the scowling, sinister-looking gentleman, Miss Jasperton."

Amilie took Fitzhugh's proffered arm and leaned in to speak to him in a stage whisper. "Is this true or a mere ruse?"

"All too true, I am afraid, and it amuses Lord Brompton to tell the story of this infamous ancestor."

Fitzhugh stopped in front of the first in the line of portraits and proceeded to reveal the name and the number of each earl as they progressed upward through all previous holders of the Brompton title.

"My Mother never spoke of them," Amilie whispered to Fitzhugh after viewing the eighth earl of Brompton.

"There are more portraits throughout the house of various and sundry of your relatives. One day I shall escort you through the rooms to view them and give their history in detail if you wish."

Amilie looked up into the face of the gentleman escorting her about the room, loud and carefree some of the time, soft and somber at others. Her heart trembled.

She sensed a deep sadness within him—a sadness he fought hard to conceal. As he pointed at the last portrait, his hand accidentally brushed her arm. Her breath caught in her throat. Her heart tapped at the walls of her chest.

"Have you discerned which one is the unfortunate one?" The present earl of Brompton's voice called out, breaking her concentration on her physical reaction to the brief touch of Fitzhugh's hand.

Amilie swiveled her eyes from portrait to portrait until she noticed Fitzhugh's concealed hand pointing to a particular frame and showing five fingers to remind Amilie of the traitor's place in the line of succession. Fitzhugh grinned, the sappy grin of someone who was amused by his own actions. Amilie giggled.

"I am guessing the fifth earl of Brompton," Amilie responded and pointed to the same portrait Fitzhugh had pointed to.

"How grand, my dear child. You have a keen eye for rascals and possess my talent for the quick discernment of bad character," the earl of Brompton said. He motioned over a footman and with an assist from the footman got to his feet. Once upright, he joined Amilie and Fitzhugh and peered through his monocle at the portraits of his ancestors. "Meek and timid is how the sixth appears here. I am sure the artist was unskilled and performed a disservice to him. Meekness and timidity are not Brompton traits—strong and valiant men they have been throughout our history. Even the fifth went to the gallows standing tall, his eyes open and his chin jutted out in defiance until the very end is the written account of his final day."

"And handsome," Lady Brompton added sidling in next to her husband, the current earl of Brompton.

A blush colored Lord Brompton's baldpate pink. Lady Brompton bent her head and kissed his cheek.

The earl of Brompton's eyes shone with tenderness. "With your flattering words, my dear, I shall retire for the night. Fitzhugh, see me to the dower house."

"Certainly, your lordship," Fitzhugh said as he removed his gaze from Amilie. "Some fresh air will be welcome. I have arranged a surprise for Miss Jasperton in the morning," he announced, nodding to her.

"I hope you did not order a replacement for Shining Star."

"Of course not, you and Shining Star are a perfect match, Miss Jasperton. I shall say no more about the surprise I have planned."

Amilie felt flushed. Why did Fitzhugh affect her in such an unpleasant manner? If she remained here after he left for London, she could concentrate on other things. Her thoughts would not be cluttered with him and her reflection on the times they were together.

After Fitzhugh and the earl of Brompton departed the drawing room, Amilie's elbow was taken in hand by Lady Brompton, who strolled with her to the door of the drawing room. "Before we part, I wish to offer a word of caution, Amilie. It is best if you resist any early flutters of attraction toward Fitzhugh. After suffering the grievous loss of your parents, you need time to gain control over your emotions before making decisions of this nature."

"My apologies if my behavior has been such it led you to believe my affections are engaged by Mr. Fitzhugh. He offered me his friendship and shared his laughter and his enthusiasm with me. His gift of friendship allowed me to forget my sorrow at times."

"Fitzhugh is leaving for London at the end of the Mullertons' visit.

"I see. I shall miss him. He has helped me discover there is still joy to be found. I am grateful."

At the top of the stairs, Lady Brompton removed her hand from Amilie's elbow and took both of Amilie's hands in hers. "I am glad you are here, Amilie. I do not wish you more heartbreak."

The words unsettled Amilie. Again she sensed something was hidden beneath. Some meaning that, despite the earl of Brompton's belief she inherited his ability for discernment, she could not envision.

Amilie tried not to let the confusion she was feeling appear on her face when she turned to look at Lady Brompton before speaking. "Your offer of shelter and protection is welcomed by me. My gratitude for your kindness is unbounded."

"And I appreciate your presence here. Your presence has provided Brompton and me great joy. Goodnight, Amilie."

Amilie opened the door to her apartments. Helaine was sitting at the table with a threaded needle in one hand and a section of the fabric of Amilie's new dress in the other. A pool of light from five burning candles surrounded her.

"Helaine, I had no idea you would be here sewing at such a late hour."

"I have finished the skirt and wished to finish the bodice for a fitting before you leave for your riding lesson tomorrow morning."

"There is no need to rush the fashioning of my new dress. I am informed the mantua-maker is to arrive by the end of the week."

"But tomorrow night, miss, there will be guests at dinner. Dinner will be very grand. Cook has been preparing for days. I want to have your dress finished for you to wear, miss."

Amilie sat down at the table. "Then we shall finish the bodice and have the fitting tonight. Tomorrow there will be less to do."

"Yes, miss. Molly, one of the parlor maids, is skilled with an embroidery needle. She has offered to help with the trim."

"I shall have to find a way to thank her." Amilie said as she threaded a needle and picked up an unfinished sleeve.

"She is pleased to help, miss."

Amilie studied the finished sleeve to see how to fashion the one in her hand. "Helaine, did you know Fitzhugh is leaving for London immediately after the Mullerton's depart?" Amilie asked. "It will be much quieter here." Amilie sniffed as tears coursed down her cheeks. She put down her sewing. "Goodness, I have no idea why I am so quick to lose my composure." She blotted her face on a scrap of facing material and picked up the sleeve again.

"No concern, miss." Helen's words were clipped, her tone curt. They concentrated on their stitches for a time. Minutes later, Amilie heard soft sniffles coming from Helaine. "I am sad he is leaving too, miss." Helaine wiped her face with her apron. "Pardon me, miss, for being out of place."

"We must not let him know of our tears, Helaine. Fitzhugh already thinks too highly of himself. I understand many ladies will be very happy when he returns to Town." Amilie laughed breaking the tension.

Ten minutes later Helaine held up the bodice. "There, we shall have your fitting now, and I shall stitch in the sleeves and be finished for the night.

Amilie took a few more stitches in the sleeve she was finishing and knotted her thread. When she entered her bedchamber, followed by Helaine, the skirt of her new dress lay across the bed waiting for a try on. The pink silk shimmered in the candlelight. Amilie picked it up. Helaine's stitches were tiny and neat and the dress had been cut out with care. The fitting showed only a minor adjustment was needed to the bodice. The skirt fit so well it would need only the final stitches.

"I will tend to my toilette tonight, Helaine. You may be excused to finish up your sewing."

"Yes, miss," Helaine said raising her hand to cover a

yawn. "The housekeeper has arranged a visit below stairs for you in the afternoon."

"Then there is a busy day ahead of me. You need not accompany me to the riding ring nor bring up breakfast tomorrow. The breakfast room is clearly marked on my maps, and once I am outside, finding the riding ring will not be difficult. When I return from my lesson, I will assist with the finish work on my new dress."

"Very good, miss. I will give these a press," Helaine said, draping the bodice and the skirt of Amilie's new dress over her arm.

Amilie slipped out of her dress and into her nightrail, sat down at the dressing table, unpinned her hair, removed the ribbon, and brushed out her curls. She reached up and snapped open the clasp of her mother's gold locket then removed the chain from around her neck. Holding the locket in the palm of one hand, she caressed the gold casing with the fingers of her other hand as if it were a talisman.

A large yawn reminded her of her need for sleep. A small crick in her back reminded her of the forgotten heated brick and liniment rub.

In the morning, Amilie entered the breakfast room to find Lord Brompton and Lady Brompton seated at the long table.

"Good morning, child," Lady Brompton said in greeting. "We are delighted you are joining us this morning."

"A glorious day for being up and about early," the earl of Brompton stated and thumped the table with his hand.

"I am happy to see you so energetic and sounding so strong this morning, Lord Brompton," Amilie said seating herself in a chair.

A footman moved forward to take her breakfast request. "Butter toast, coffee, and marmalade." she said as she unfolded the serviette and spread it across her lap. "And a boiled egg," she called in a raised voice to the footman's back.

The earl of Brompton cleared his throat. "I am feeling much like my old self. Robust. Hearty. Full of spring sap. My rigging in good repair and my sails filled by a steady wind."

Amilie laughed. "A wonderful description of good health."

"And how are you getting on, child?"

"I am enjoying my new adventures."

"Good to hear. Good to hear. Parliament is opening soon and we shall be off to adventures in London."

Amilie's happy facial expression turned into a frown.

Lady Brompton thumped the table with her fist, sat up straight, and shot the earl of Brompton a fierce look. "I am sure you look forward to being surrounded by your peers, Brompton. I am not sure if I will be joining you in London this time."

The earl of Brompton pushed out his bottom lip in a pout. He busied himself with a piece of bread, cleaning the egg yolk from his plate. "Quite right, my dear.

Quite right," he said as he placed the palms of his hands flat on the tabletop and pushed himself to his feet. Then gripping the knobbed handle of his walking stick, he hobbled from the breakfast room.

Watching Amilie break small pieces from a slice of butter toast and dropping them back unto her plate, Lady Brompton spoke to her in a measured and calm voice.

"Eat your breakfast, child. You need the strength for your riding lesson. Do not upset yourself over thoughts of London. Unless it is your desire to go, you and I shall remain here and let Fitzhugh tend to Brompton this time."

Amilie looked into Lady Brompton's soft, concerned eyes. "After I have the experience of our guests and take part in the entertainments you have planned, the thought of London and mingling with the *ton* may not seem so daunting."

Amilie finished eating a full slice of her toasted bread, spread thick with the marmalade, and emptied her coffee cup. "The clock shows I must soon be off to the riding ring."

"Enjoy your lesson today. I have sent word to the stable to ready my horse. I plan a long ride today, perhaps as far as the hills."

Amilie dabbed at her lips then brushed a crumb from her bodice. "And thank you for arranging a tour below stairs for me. My imagination lacks the ability to picture the expanse of rooms Helaine has described.

"It is impressive below stairs. I think after seeing all the activity that goes on below our feet you will gain an

Susan Ralph

understanding of the great effort that is involved in maintaining such a large home. Now, before I enjoy my ride, I must finish the last of the invitations for the ball in honor of the Mullertons. Then this afternoon I must complete the arrangements for the assembly we sponsor when the Mullertons visit, and Cook is threatening to quit if I don't meet with her to plan the food for the annual picnic at the lake."

Lady Brompton reached over and patted Amilie's hand. "We both have a busy day ahead. Shall we get started?"

Chapter Eleven

As Amilie neared the riding ring, she noticed the groom and Shining Star standing outside the fence that surrounded it. She slowed her pace, wondering why they had not gone inside where they had waited on other days.

And there was a second horse tethered to the fence nuzzling the groom's hand. Partially hidden behind the groom, Fitzhugh sat atop a red-hued chestnut, leaning over in the saddle and patting the horse's neck. *What was the meaning of this odd tableau?*

Fitzhugh swung his long legs over his horse and dismounted. *Was this his surprise?* Amilie's nerves threatened to overtake the confidence she had built up over the past few days.

"Why is everyone outside the ring this morning?" she called.

"Part of the surprise I promised you last evening, Miss Jasperton. Today we are following one of the riding trails that run through the grounds."

If Fitzhugh intended to tease her, his actions were cruel. She wanted to spin around and return to the safety of the Manor house, but she could not move. She swiveled her eyes to study the groom.

The groom nodded his head in the affirmative.

"I will ride ahead of you," Fitzhugh said. His manner was that of a man used to command. His voice allowed no doubt. "The path is wide enough for the groom to ride alongside you."

"But, I am not ready."

"I had a good talk with Shining Star this morning and informed her she is to behave."

Amilie removed a glove and rubbed her bare hand the length of Shining Star's nose. The mare's soft, brown eyes managed to convey to Amilie she could trust her.

Amilie gave a skittish laugh then gritted her teeth, placed her hand in Fitzhugh's and swung into the saddle.

"Straighten your back like I showed you, miss," the groom said as he made a final check of Amilie and Shining Star. Amilie adjusted her hips and shoulders as the groom's critical eye watched. Then, with a nod of his head, the groom handed her the reins. The three riders started moving toward a distant tree line.

Shining Star kept to an easy, rhythmic gait as she followed behind Fitzhugh's horse. After only a short distance, the sway of the horse lulled Amilie; her confidence returned, her breathing slowed, her eyes focused again. She could see the wildflowers that were blooming this time of year, adding their dots of color to the brown and green floor of the woodlands. Her ears unblocked, and she could hear the birds making announcements to one another. Riding slowly atop a horse allowed a larger view than when she was on foot and still allowed her the time to absorb the beauty of the surroundings.

Fitzhugh adjusted himself in his saddle and looked back at Amilie. "How are you doing, Miss Jasperton?"

"Wonderful, Mr. Fitzhugh. I am pleased you thought to plan this surprise for me."

The path the three riders were taking circled them around to a open area where a grass covered dome bulged out of the ground and two parallel brick walls guarded steps that descended into the earth.

"Your education and my surprise continue, Miss Jasperton." Fitzhugh dismounted and took up a position next to Shining Star to assist Amilie's dismount.

The groom took the reins of all three horses and led them to an area where they could graze.

"What is this, Mr. Fitzhugh?" Amilie said gesturing toward the steps.

"Come see." Fitzhugh motioned to Amilie to follow as he started down the steps. Stopping his descent on the third step, he faced her and held out both of his hand. "Careful, Miss Jasperton, the steps are slippery with moss."

Amilie took Fitzhugh's hand innocently enough. But

as his fingers closed around hers, all of her senses rolled up into a single awareness, giving her the perception of being completed. Their hands fit together as precisely as the scribed edges of her dissected puzzle pieces. When the pieces of her puzzle were fitted together in proper order, they formed a map of England. What might be formed if she and Fitzhugh were fitted together as pieces of the same puzzle?

Shaken by her reaction to this light coupling of their hands, and with Lady Brompton's warning to guard against any feelings stronger than friendship echoing in her mind, Amilie withdrew her hand and backed away.

"Where does this stairway lead, Mr. Fitzhugh," she asked. Her voice sounded whispery and timorous to her ears.

"Trust me, Miss Jasperton," he replied in the same commanding voice he used to reassure her about riding outside the ring. "You have a reluctance to follow until you know the destination," Fitzhugh said, laughing at his own statement.

"After the stories of your misadventures, you fault me for being cautious?" Amilie said letting the tightness of her shoulders loosen and taking deeper breaths.

"I am reformed of my desire for risky adventures. You need not fear my placing you in jeopardy."

Amilie lifted her right foot, moved back to the top of the stairs, and grabbed the handrail built into the side of the wall. "Your testament to Shining Star's behavior proved true. I will trust your word about my safety here." Amilie presented him a weak smile.

At the bottom of the steps, Fitzhugh tugged at the handle of a solid wood door. The forged, iron hinges groaned as the door swung outward. Amilie peered into the dim interior. Bricks formed the walls and ceiling of the vaulted, cave-like area. Stepping inside, Fitzhugh pulled the door closed behind them. The cool, damp air forced chill bumps on any area of exposed skin. Amilie shivered, crossing her arms over her chest. Fitzhugh placed his arm around her shoulders and pulled her to his side.

"The ice house, Miss Jasperton. Built to preserve harvested ice for lengthy periods of time so we might savor our ices and enjoy our frozen creams."

The nape of Amilie's neck heated as though someone had placed a hot poker there. The sensation of warmth radiated outward and downward, spreading through her entire body; the places where her hip and shoulder pressed against Fitzhugh's leg and chest sizzled and steamed like water spattered over a hot pan.

"Well, this has been an education," she said in a strained, chirpy voice as she moved forward and to the side to disengage from their physical contact. She fussed with her skirt to avoid looking at him and moved to the door. Grunting from the weight, she pushed the door open enough to slip through the narrow slit and started up the steps. "I am to be given a tour below stairs today," she called over her shoulder. She hurried up the steps to get into the fresh air and clear her head. "My visit here fits nicely."

"We do fit well together." Fitzhugh said after catching up with her as she headed toward the groom and the horses.

A rush of heat flooded Amilie's cheeks. She kept her face directed away from Fitzhugh's eyes. She did not care to enhance his amusement by showing him the discomfort he caused her with his intimate words.

The groom was sitting beneath a tree and leaning back against the trunk. Amilie bustled toward him calling for his assistance in mounting Shining Star.

Atop their respective horses, the three riders retraced the trail. All of the joy Amilie experienced earlier dissolved into maudlin thoughts. Fitzhugh would soon be gone from Brompton Manor. Her heart sank, at the same time a feeling of relief washed through her. He would be out of sight and there would be no chance for inadvertent physical contact between them. Yet again, someone who had engaged her heart would leave her.

Dismounting, Amilie kept her eyes on Shining Star. She put her face close to the mare's neck and patted and murmured to her.

"I am off for a longer ride. Thank Helaine for the timing of your activities today," Fitzhugh said and waved his hand. He turned his horse, preparing to set off down the carriage lane.

"You and Helaine conspired together to plan my day?" Amilie managed a laugh and found the courage to look at him.

Leaving her question unanswered, Fitzhugh touched the brim of his hat, and set his horse into motion. Amilie stared at his backside as he kicked his horse into a gallop.

When he was out of sight, she patted Shining Star once more, laid her head against the warmth of the mare's neck for a moment, then handed her reins to the groom and headed for the Manor house. Everything changed so fast, changed before one could get their bearing and feel secure again. Troubling thoughts disturbed her ease as she meandered along the path back to the Manor house.

Amilie removed her gloves and hat and hurried up the staircase and along the hall to her apartments.

In the sitting room, Helaine sat near a window, stitching a piece of the pink silk.

After ordering Helaine to keep at her work and not get up, Amilie stowed her outdoor items in the proper place in her bedchamber and returned to the sitting room. She picked up a small chair and placed it next to Helaine. "How may I be of help, Helaine?" she asked sitting down.

"The bodice is finished, miss, except for the trim. I am almost finished with this ruffle to edge the bottom of the skirt."

"I see Molly has scattered lovely embroidered flowers about the skirt fabric. She is as skilled as you promised."

"Molly and me perfected our needle skills over years of helping the mantua-maker."

"Molly lived here as a child too?"

"Yes, miss. Her father is head groom. Molly and me are as close as true sisters would be."

"I believe the two of you are skilled enough for a shop of your own."

"Thank you, miss. I have no knowledge of how to go about opening a shop."

"Well, if you had a shop, you would have to leave behind everything familiar and comfortable to you."

"Yes, miss."

"Can Molly read?"

"She can, miss. I taught her after Mr. Fitzhugh taught me."

Amilie pulled a chair up to the window and pushed a length of thread through the eye of a needle. She picked up a piece of trim from a box full of odds and ends sitting on the table next to Helaine. "This lace is exquisite, Helaine, so wispy and delicate. Should I add some around the neckline and the bottom of the sleeves, to soften them? Perhaps there is enough here for a double row along the edge of the sleeves."

"A fine idea, miss."

Amilie set to her work, totally focused on her stitches until shouts from the courtyard intruded and disturbed the peaceful atmosphere in the sitting room.

"Tom. Come quick. Hurry lad." Orders boomed forth in a voice that could only be Fitzhugh's.

"Cannot Mr. Fitzhugh take his horse to the stables and refrain from shouting in the courtyard for assistance?" Amilie asked.

"He could, miss. But he favors Tom and slips him a treat when he comes 'round to take the horse."

"I see. I suppose it is impossible to give Tom his treat in the stable yard."

"The grooms don't like it, miss. They think Tom might get spoiled and take advantage."

Amilie lifted her head and sighed as the shouts continued.

"Tom prepare, lad. The enemy is near and gaining rapidly." Fitzhugh's cry of alarm sailed through the window glass.

"Yes sir. Ready to defend the horses, sir," came an equally loud voice in response.

Amilie lay aside her sewing and stood up to look out from her window and down into the courtyard. Fitzhugh swung his leg over his horse. The sight of the graceful arc made by his long leg stirred her senses. She moved away from the window and plopped back down in her chair.

"Handsome and charming, miss. All of the ladies say so about him."

"What is he shouting about? Why is he alerting Tom that the enemy is approaching and to prepare to defend? Every time I begin to understand this place something new arises to confuse me."

"He must have seen the carriages bearing the Mullertons coming along the road—calls them the enemy since he was a lad, he does."

Amilie resumed sewing and changed the subject.

"Mr. Fitzhugh had a grand surprise for me today. He arranged for me to ride Shining Star outside of the riding ring."

"Really, miss?"

"I found riding at a slow pace as grand as walking."

Helaine raised her head from her sewing and looked at her mistress. "When Mr. Fitzhugh leaves for London, a groom will chaperone your rides."

"I plan to ride every day. Shining Star is my one true friend here, and she will never leave me."

"People do love their animals, miss."

"I believe you and Mr. Fitzhugh conspired to plan my surprise."

Helaine's face colored. She lowered her head. "I hope you are not angry, miss."

"I enjoyed the visit to the ice house, and I learned a valuable lesson."

Helaine rose to her feet and busied herself securing her needle and folding the skirt section. "The ruffle needs a press, then the bodice can be attached to the skirt when you are finished with the lace."

"And my new dress will be my shield when I meet the enemy tonight." Amilie laughed merrily and held the dress bodice away from her to study the effect of the lace trim. "Mr. Fitzhugh possesses a lively imagination, but if his warning is true, and the Mullertons are the enemy, I will be prepared."

Helaine covered her mouth, but not soon enough to stop a series of giggles from sounding.

Amilie concentrated on her work. Contentment settled around her as she engaged in an activity that was familiar to her.

The clatter of wheels and the strike of horses' hooves hitting cobblestones announced the arrival of Fitzhugh's enemies. Amilie lay aside her sewing and stood to one side of her window, partially concealing herself with the aid of the curtain.

The three guests emerged from the lead carriage, stretching their legs and smoothing down their clothing as they touched the ground.

There was no outward indication of their status as the enemy. No weapons, no regimental adornments, their dress was what one would expect. The lady was adorned with feathers and tulle; the two gentlemen wore tailored jackets, light-colored breeches, and polished boots.

"Stop nattering," the older gentleman said in a rather loud voice. "My head is in a swirl from your endless and senseless chattering."

The woman next to him leaned over and touched the older gentleman's arm. The countess of Brompton came down the steps with her spine straight, her shoulders back, and her chin held high. She swept gracefully downward until she stood in the flat of the courtyard.

Mrs. Mullerton, the future countess of Brompton, hurried forward. The ladies kissed one another's cheeks and then the current countess of Brompton turned to greet the two gentlemen. She offered her hand to the elder gentleman and then to the younger.

Amilie took three steps back from the window as the group started toward the entrance steps.

A flurry of footman swarmed into the courtyard and began to unload the portmanteaus, wood boxes of all shapes and sizes, valises, and several hatboxes from the two conveyances.

After the courtyard cleared, Amilie settled back into her chair, pinned the second layer of lace around the edge of the right sleeve, and began stitching it to the dress.

Fitzhugh's enemies certainly appeared tame, but perhaps the wiser course involved a more careful examination of their character before she decided for herself whether they were friend or foe.

Helaine brought Amilie's lunch tray, placed the dishes on the table, picked up the dress bodice, and admired Amilie's work. "'Tis exactly the thing, miss. This trim."

Amilie sat down to eat and retrieved her bible from the stack of books.

"Do you attend church services, Helaine?"

"Oh, yes, miss. 'most every Sunday. His lordship insists. A small staff always stays behind to watch over the Manor house, but the rest are expected at morning service unless we are so ill we can't leave our bed."

"Honor thy Father and thy Mother we are told. I hope I remember always to honor mine." Amilie heard a pensive tone in her voice.

"And I too, miss. Me mum, I mean. Now best we be on our way down the stairs for your tour. The housekeeper is as particular about people being on time as her ladyship is."

The two young women traversed a route to arrive at the landing in front of Mrs. Burton's door at the agreed upon time. Helaine tapped on the door in front of them.

"Miss," the housekeeper offered when she opened the door. She executed a respectful curtsy unlike their first encounter, but she retained the dour expression on her face.

"Mrs. Burton, how kind of you to show me the workings below stairs," Amilie said, smiling.

"And on our busiest day, miss. But come along."

Mrs. Burton led the way down the remainder of the steps landing them in a small antechamber. Taking a key from among the many hooked to the chatelaine at her waist, she unlocked a door in the far wall and stepped aside so Amilie could enter. Wood cabinets and shelves left no wall space barren. A long, wooden table sat in the center of the room. "The china and silver are stored here, miss. Only the butler and me carries a key for this room. Every dish and every piece of silver used at a meal is counted and cleaned in here."

Amilie could see large silver urns and several tall candelabra stored on shelves behind glass-paned doors. The three reversed course. Mrs. Burton turned the key in the lock, testing the door handle, then led the way down a short hall into a large room as busy as a village center on market day. Women, their dresses covered with white, bibbed aprons and mobcaps pulled tight over their hair were stirring pots and chopping vegetables. A red-faced women stood near the fire poking a long-handled fork into roasts on the spit. One woman cracked eggs into a bowl, another peeled apples. Tins, waiting to be filled, were lined up along a table.

Amilie heard herself gasp. The size of Brompton Manor's kitchen, with workspace for the fifteen kitchen workers she counted and with a fireplace cooking area equal to half the size of her sitting room, startled her.

"Cook has agreed to show you how she prepares her frozen cream. Her ladyship ordered it served for to-night's dinner."

Cook gave the party a warm, welcoming smile when they invaded her special domain. She reached under the wooden table and brought out two pewter basins—one larger than the other. Then, she bent down and pulled out a lid that fit the smaller basin.

"Too early to start making the frozen cream. Don't hold well. But here is how 'tis done."

Amilie listened and watched while Cook proceeded with her demonstration. "When 'tis the time, I send the scullery boy to the ice house for my ice and set him to the task of chipping it. Then I pour my cream, fresh from the milk cows this very morning, into the smaller basin, add sugar and my choice of fruit, then cover the basin close with the lid and sit it in the larger basin. The extra space in the large basin, I fill up with the chipped ice and toss on a handful of salt."

"And the ice is cold enough to freeze the cream?"

" 'Tis, miss. The cream is stirred after it sets a spell, then more ice and salt is added and it sets for a longer time."

"I am looking forward to my first taste of frozen cream."

"Then I will take extra care to make it good and proper, miss."

The housekeeper continued on with the tour, opening doors into storerooms of varying sizes and listing the items stored there. The stillroom, the scullery, the laundry and pressing room, and the wine cellar all came under scrutiny before the tour ended.

Amilie thanked the housekeeper, who dipped a little deeper curtsy than the one she made at the beginning of the tour. Even her facial expression had softened.

As they headed toward the stairs, the clatter of tins preceded two young maids into the anteroom. Jostling one another and giggling, they stopped abruptly. Their mouths dropped open.

The housekeeper scowled at them and spoke with a frosty tone. "Come to my room as soon as you pick up and store your pails."

Amilie watched as the two maids dipped deep curtsies, picked up the pails, and scurried off. Then she and Helaine headed back to the main part of the house. "Mrs. Burton didn't show you the room in which we take our meals, miss. The room is very nice; her ladyship insists. And we work all the harder because of it."

"I see there is a lot of work that needs doing and why a large staff is required."

"And even more work when there are guests. The two maids, banging down the stairs, are two of the chambermaids. Their duties increase greatly when guest apartments are in use."

Helaine pulled a folded sheet of paper from her apron pocket. "I made a list of the servants' names and their positions." Helaine handed the paper to Amilie. "The butler and the housekeeper are at the top. They see to everything that goes on inside the house. Since there are no children, there is no governess or tutor; but if there were, they would be separate from the household staff. His lordship's valet and her ladyship's lady's maid are under supervision of the one they serve. But everyone else inside the house is the butler and the housekeeper's responsibility."

"Do you find your relationship with the others below stairs is changed now that you have moved up?"

"Yes, miss. If I may be bold."

"Are you unhappy because of this?"

"No, miss. To serve you is a pleasure. I am adjusting to my new place in the household."

"And Mr. Fitzhugh's valet?"

"The head footman is serving as valet to him for the short period of time he will be here."

"You and Mr. Fitzhugh are good conspirators, Helaine. Today has been full of wonderful educational events."

A big grin split Helaine's face. "Ever since our childhood. We trust each other, miss."

"And when he is gone away, you miss him?"

"Very much, miss."

Chapter Twelve

Helaine fastened the back of Amilie's dress and stepped aside. Her hand covered her mouth. "Oh, miss."

Amilie stood in front of the cheval glass. "Helaine, the dress fits perfectly."

The thin, soft silk fell from the high-waist bodice of the dress, skimmed Amilie's hips, and ended in the narrow ruffle Helaine had fashioned and attached at the hem. The roses Molly embroidered were the perfect accent for the pink fabric. The lace trim circling the edge of the sleeves and around the deep-cut neckline of the dress softened the transition between the fabric and the bare skin of Amilie's arms and chest.

"My purchase was extravagant, but has proven a wise choice in your skilled hands."

" 'Twas a pleasure, miss."

"I am fully armored and ready to face Fitzhugh's enemies. Perhaps I can help him in his defense."

"He has long experience with the Mullertons. I think he is prepared to defend hisself."

Amilie pulled open the top drawer of her dressing table. "I think my gold locket is suitable."

"Yes, miss, the perfect addition." Helaine secured the clasp on the locket's chain at the back of Amilie's neck, removed a small box from a pocket in her dress, and lifted the lid. "Her ladyship sent a pair of gold and diamond earrings for you to wear if you wish."

Amilie looked into the box, picked up one of the earrings, and held the sparkling adornment at her earlobe. She stared into her looking-glass. "Perhaps these are intended to draw attention away from my old, unfashionable dress this evening."

"Her ladyship don't concern herself none about impressing the Mullertons." Helaine dropped her eyes. "I beg pardon, miss. Her ladyship's concerns are not for me to say."

"You need not apologize, Helaine. Your knowledge about these matters is welcome."

After fastening the earrings to Amilie's ears, Helaine studied Amilie's reflection in the looking-glass. "You are a sight to see, miss. I wonder at the reaction when you appear in the drawing room."

"Express my compliments to Molly for her embroidery work. I promise to detail her ladyship's reaction for you when I return this evening."

"And his lordship's and Mr. Fitzhugh's reactions too, please."

Amilie inhaled a deep breath, ventured into the hall-way, and gained the cross-hall that connected to the main staircase, at the same time Fitzhugh came out the hall door of his rooms.

Colin Fitzhugh eyed the young woman. His eyes fixated on her as she moved toward him. "Miss Jasperton. I believe."

"Who else might I be, Mr. Fitzhugh?"

"I thought, for a time, you were the ghost of a guest who dressed for dinner, set out for the drawing room, became lost, and still wanders the halls of this bewildering maze of a building."

"You tease. Mr. Fitzhugh. However, your eyes are deceived if you think I am amorphous. What appears a flimsy dinner dress is in truth a solid suit of armor donned to protect against the weapons of the enemy. After I overheard your warning to Tom, I prepared myself to help defend the castle."

Fitzhugh clutched his mid-section with both hands and roared with laughter.

"I fear no pistol shots or arrows will be repelled by your dress, Miss Jasperton. However, fear not, I am trained to rescue fair maidens who wear dainty dresses from attackers."

Fitzhugh formed his face into a fierce scowl.

Amilie drew herself up to her tallest height and

squared her shoulders. "Perhaps my real armor is concealed beneath and is not visible to the eye."

Fitzhugh instantly sobered. "I beg pardon, Miss Jasperton," he said and made a small bow. "Now if you will excuse me, I believe a return to my rooms to don a suit of chain mall capable of warding off the sword thrusts from well-armored ladies, is in order."

Fitzhugh's hand brushed Amilie's hand as he tried to move around her. Tingles rippled upward and across the nape of her neck then down her other arm. Her bravado shattered into a million pieces. She took a small step to her right to find Fitzhugh had moved in the same direction. Her vision centered on his colorful waistcoat. Then her eyes, as though attached to strings in the hands of a puppet master, moved upward until they were filled by the intensity in his eyes. The recognition of a familiarity, her deep comfort with this gentleman, swelled her heart.

Fitzhugh raised his hand to touch her mother's small gold locket resting against the exposed skin above the neckline of her dress. His finger grazed her flesh; the touch burning as though a spark from the fire grate had struck her. She needed to move aside, to move back, to escape from his alluring presence. She could not.

"You have worn this locket to dinner each evening, Miss Jasperton." His voice was husky. His breath soft and sweet.

"It was my mother's."

Amilie's words came out in a whisper—her entire being intent on the closeness of him. His face descended towards hers, she stretched upward to meet him. His warm breath caressed her cheek; his soft lips touched hers, she strained to meet him, pressing her lips tight against his. The open space around her disappeared, nothing mattered, only the rightness of their kiss and the warmth that enveloped her.

"Miss Jasperton. Mr. Fitzhugh." Helaine's voice echoed down the long hall. The tray, she was carrying, fell from her hands. The items sitting atop the tray tumbled and clattered along the hall floor.

Fitzhugh jumped back, fingered his cravat, and skewed the perfection of the tie into a crumpled mess. Amilie bowed her head, tugged the lace at the neckline of her dress, and took several steps backwards until the wall prevented her from moving back any farther.

"Helaine." Fitzhugh cleared his throat several times, then with a nod of his head to Helaine and Amilie, disappeared through the door of his rooms, slamming the door behind him.

Amilie watched Helaine hurrying down the hall toward her, then covered her face with her hands and concentrated on quieting her breathing.

"Miss?" Helaine was gasping.

Amilie dropped her hands but kept her eyes on the carpet. "This time I shall not reconsider, Helaine." Her voice had strengthened with a new resolve. "Pack my valises. Tomorrow I intend to purchase a ticket for the next post coach. My ability to resist Mr. Fitzhugh's allure is no longer in question."

"'Tis Mr. Fitzhugh's fault over this." Helaine said followed by the sound of a chocked back sob.

"I fear this is my fault, Helaine. I was cautioned against desiring more than a friendship with Mr. Fitzhugh. I tried to abide the warning, but I lose all reason when I am near him."

"Yes, miss." Helaine pulled herself to her full height. "Perhaps Mr. Fitzhugh will return to London earlier then was planned. Now, if I may be bold, it is time you go down to meet his lordship's guests."

Amilie felt Helaine's nudge and moved away from the wall. As she moved to the top of the grand staircase, Helaine remained by her side, steadying her.

Amilie took in a deep breath and spoke softly, as though speaking only to herself. "I shall visit the squire and his family. Time at Brompton Manor is important to Mr. Fitzhugh. This is his home, not mine. I shall be the one to leave."

At the top of the staircase, Amilie paused, folded her hands together, and bowed her neck.

Helaine spoke in a soft, reassuring voice. "Mr. Fitzhugh will control his passions, miss. If I may be bold in saying so. Now down the stairs with you. Shoulders back and remember you promised to tell me about her ladyship's reaction to your dress. No need now to describe Mr. Fitzhugh's reaction." Helaine covered her mouth with her hands, but not before the sound of her laughter made Amilie smile.

Amilie lifted her chin and stepped onto the first step. "My new armor offered me no protection against the charms of a fellow solider. I do hope it is more effective against the enemy."

Helaine watched as Amilie descended the steps then made her way back to Amilie's sitting room, sat down at the writing desk and inked a note.

Mr. Fitzhugh,
If you break Miss Jasperton's heart, my Calendula ointment is not strong enough to mend it.

Helaine

She went along the hall to Fitzhugh's rooms, pushed the folded paper through the sliver of space at the bottom of the door, then scurried off in the direction of the servant's staircase.

"Miss Amilie Jasperton," the liveried footman announced in full, rounded tones to the current occupants of the drawing room.

Amilie placed a smile on her face and crossed the threshold. Lady Brompton came toward her, and as she had previously, met her in the center of the room and took her elbow. She leaned over to whisper. "Dearest Amilie. Your dress is perfection. I am pleased by your surprise. Such a clever child, you are. When we are alone, you must tell me how you managed."

The earl of Brompton occupied his usual chair, his hands flailing about to punctuate the story he was telling.

Lady Brompton interrupted the earl of Brompton's animated discourse.

His face fell into a scowl. "I am nearing the exciting part of my story," the earl of Brompton said, and sputtered.

"I am sure the highwaymen are content to wait while I present Amilie to our guests."

Amilie executed her best deep curtsy. "My apology for my arrival at this inopportune moment and interrupting your story, Lord Brompton."

The earl of Brompton's eyes scanned Amilie from head to toe. "I forgive you, my dear. You look delightful this evening. After the introductions are made, I shall issue an order that a footman watch over you, 'round the clock, while an unwed gentleman is in residence." The earl of Brompton swiveled his eyes to George Mullerton and glowered.

Lady Brompton presented Amilie to each of the Mullertons' in turn. Amilie sensed their coolness toward her, but she smiled and curtsied in her best manner.

The earl of Brompton's comment about assigning a footman to guard her when an unwed gentleman was in residence puzzled her. No footman had been assigned to watch over her night and day while the unmarried Fitzhugh was in residence. What was she to make of that? And why would she need protection from George Mullerton and not from Mr. Fitzhugh? As soon as she thought she had the answer to a question, another question, even more baffling, popped up.

"Mr. Colin Fitzhugh." The footman's announcement

broke the tension that the earl of Brompton's pointed ·
remark created.

Fitzhugh's manner appeared subdued as he made
his way across the room. His stride was shorter than
usual, the expression in his eyes was flat, the smile on
his lips wry.

The earl of Brompton gestured to a footman who
moved to his side. Lord Brompton held out his arm,
and clutching the footman's arm, rose to his feet and
glared at Fitzhugh. "Greet our guests, and explain why
you are late again."

Fitzhugh bowed and, as commanded, greeted each of
the Mullertons then directed his attention to Lord
Brompton.

"Your lordship," he said and made a deep bow. "It is
my deepest regret that my arrival this evening was delayed. I fear my battle wounds prevented me from ac-
complishing a hurried toilette."

The earl of Brompton sat back down. "Your cravat is
disreputable. After the disaster the other evening, I ordered my valet to instruct your man in the art of tying a
cravat. I see no progress has been made."

"My man accomplished a fine tie, but in my haste to
arrive in the drawing room on time, a small stumble on
the stair caused me to disturb his good work."

Amilie bit down on her bottom lip in an effort to prevent the laughter bubbling in her chest from spurting
out. George eyed Fitzhugh with a scornful look. The
older Mullertons' adjusted their own clothing and kept
their eyes averted, Lady Brompton snapped open her

fan and fanned herself with quick flutters of the un-furled silk.

A collective sigh of relief sounded when the earl of Brompton slapped his leg, threw back his head, and roared with laughter. "Perhaps a sedan chair is required to carry you from your room to the drawing room each evening, Fitzhugh. Ever since your return, you seem in-capable of managing the short journey on time and without mishap."

George huffed in a large quantity of air and moved to offer Amilie his arm. Standing next to George, her chin floated above his head. Fitzhugh followed, at the rear of the procession.

Lady Brompton seated George to the right of Amilie and Mr. Mullerton to her left. Fitzhugh was seated di-rectly across the table from George. He was examaning and rearranging the eating utensils at his place setting.

Amilie dreaded the necessity of carrying on a dia-logue with her table partners and prayed the gentleman would provide the conversation while she concentrated on keeping her eyes averted from Fitzhugh. His kiss had so disturbed her emotions; she feared she would giggle hysterically or weep copious tears if she caught his eye.

As a diversion, she began to count the pieces making up the elaborate table decoration. Fashioned in silver, the intricate figures were spread along the length of a mirrored tray; horses with riders, some standing in place, some jumping across obstacles, some in full pursuit, followed a pack of dogs. The silver pieces included hedgerows, thickets of trees, fences, and buildings.

"I see you eyeing the centerpiece, Miss Jasperton." George said to Amilie in a proprietary manner. He gave a sweep of his hand toward the centerpiece, proclaiming this his favorite of the numerous centerpieces available for display at Brompton Manor.

"I am looking for the fox," Amilie said.

"The fox is elusive. Never found in the same spot."

"How marvelous."

"Are you a hunter, Miss Jasperton?"

"Oh no." Amilie covered her chest with her hand and widened her eyes. "I believe it is cruel to chase after animals for sport."

"Disappointing."

A loud snort sounded from across the table. Fitzhugh covered his mouth with his fist and coughed.

"Perhaps thinking it cruel is only natural for a young lady of your experience," George said. His words were spoken in a superior tone.

Amilie made no reply and did not look up. The innuendo George had made about her limited upbringing penetrated her armor. The sting of the barb was real.

George cut a large piece of beef from the slice on his plate and shoveled the meat into his mouth. The sound of his teeth masticating the beef ground away at Amilie's heart.

Mr. Mullerton covered her silence as he launched into his observations of the intricate workings of a steam-powered machine being marketed by Watt and Boulton, declaring this new technology was capable of revolutionizing the world by replacing the labor of large numbers of the horses and men, while at the same time increasing the production of goods.

The earl of Brompton's attention focused on his cousin's description of the workings of this new machine while the others, seated at the table, were held hostage to the two gentlemen's spirited, high-volume conversation.

To change her perspective and avoid looking toward Fitzhugh, Amilie turned her eyes to Mrs. Mullerton, who was busy looking intently at one item on the table and then another as though calculating the worth of each piece with the zeal of a pawnshop owner. Perhaps her assessment of Mrs. Mullerton's interest in adding up the value of the table and its contents was unfair, but speculating on the future countess of Brompton's thoughts prevented her from blushing at the memory of Fitzhugh's lips touching hers.

After the second remove, Lady Brompton tapped her wine glass with her spoon. "We are to enjoy a special treat tonight in honor of our guests."

The butler clapped his hands, gathering the attention of everyone at the table. A footman entered the dining room through the door to the service area carrying a large silver tray with a frosted silver bowl in the center and several thick glass dishes surrounding the bowl. He sat it in the center of a small serving table.

All eyes were on the butler as he spooned pink,

frozen cream into the shallow indentation in the individual glass dishes. The footman then went around the table placing a filled glass in front of each person seated at the table.

Amilie picked up her spoon and dipped into the creamy concoction. The first taste of frozen cream dissolved in the warmth of her mouth, coated her tongue and left behind the perfume of fruit.

"Strawberries." The earl of Brompton licked his lips. "One marvels over the advances and discoveries of our botanists and horticulturists. Why we need machinery to speed our lives is incomprehensible. Life at the current speed is exactly right. No one needs to rush about any faster than they do at present and an increased production of goods will only serve to overflow the shops."

"Balderdash Brompton," Mullerton said, spooning up the last of his frozen cream. "Improvement in the ways of making things allows for an ease of living for everyone."

"It is my intent to live long enough to see the results of this new fangled steam power. I predict it will fail and no one will benefit."

"God forbid, you should miss this, Brompton," Mullerton said followed by a snort.

The earl of Brompton harrumphed and ran his spoon around the sides of the glass that had held the frozen cream, then licked the spoon.

Everyone exclaimed about the frozen cream and the talents of Brompton Manor's cook. Lady Brompton rose and led the ladies to the drawing room.

Seated in the drawing room, Amilie listened to and

studied the conversation between Mrs. Mullerton and Lady Brompton as they savored their tea and spoke of the details of running the house. Then they began to talk of mutual acquaintances, with Mrs. Mullerton repeating the latest gossip circulating in London. When their conversation changed to the latest fashions and fabrics, Mrs. Mullerton turned to Amilie.

"My dear Miss Jasperton, I have been admiring the fabric of your dress all evening. May I ask where you purchased such exquisite goods?"

"From the mercer in the village, a Mr. White. I am told he was once established in London."

Amilie's answer extracted an indigent sounding grunt from Mrs. Mullerton's rouged lips.

"Why, I patronized Mr. White's London shop for years. Every time I found myself in town, which was often, I made substantial purchases at his shop. Then one year, I arrived at the address to find him gone. Imagine my upset. Most disrespectful of him to relocate and not send notice to his most loyal customer."

"We were pleased he chose to open a shop in our village. When he mentioned he was desirous of a quieter place to live, and subsequently I learned he was born and raised in this part of England, I enticed him to move his establishment here."

"And never spoke a word of it to me."

"You never once mentioned to me your patronage of Mr. White's shop. I knew of no reason to mention to you he moved his shop here."

"I see he still has a keen eye for colors that flatter," Mrs. Mullerton said. She was still eyeing Amilie's dress as she accepted a second cup of tea and helped herself to a small biscuit from the plate on the table near her seat. "Who was the mantua-maker who fashioned the dress? I wonder at the local talent."

"I . . . ," Amilie began. But before she could credit Helaine and Molly, Lady Brompton rattled her teacup in its saucer.

"The dress is lovely," Lady Brompton said, then set her teacup down and swiveled her head to face Mrs. Mullerton. "Amilie has received no instruction in dance. I have engaged an excellent dance master and his wife who will arrive tomorrow. I expect George is agreeable to partner with Amilie during her lessons."

Mrs. Mullerton swallowed the last of the biscuit. "I shall insist." She turned to look at Amilie. "Miss Jasperton, you are fortunate to have my son here to assist you. There is no dance partner more skilled than George. Why the young ladies, at Almack's, crowd around him when he arrives. Their mothers often express to me a desire to have George partner with their daughter." Mrs. Mullerton twittered. "I believe they mean they desire for George to offer for their daughter, but George is particular. I have wasted my time trying to prompt him toward the highly favorable Lady Mary Walden and have pointed out to him other agreeable young ladies, but he ignores my promptings and remains free of commitment."

Amilie sipped her tea and tried to keep any reaction to Mrs. Mullerton's remarks from showing on her face. Nothing said tonight would be of any consequence, if she decided to leave in the morning.

Chapter Thirteen

The sun was playing hide-and-seek with the gathering clouds when Amilie arrived for her riding lesson. Today the groom accompanied her on her ride, leading her along an unfamiliar riding trail.

As the horses carried them over gentle hills and across wide expanses of grasslands, a mist rose from the warm, damp earth and swirled about the horses' hooves and fetlocks. Amilie was enchanted by the trail's beauty, the serenity and the aura of mysticism. But the silence, in the absence of Fitzhugh's good humor and energy, set a pall over the day.

She comforted her loneliness by concentrating on the gentle sway of the horse beneath her. Though the mare could not speak words, she could communicate trust and warmth and friendship.

Back at the riding ring, Amilie quickly mastered the

physical command and the rhythm of the new gait the groom taught. As Shining Star trotted around the ring for the second time, Amilie saw George standing outside the ring. He leaned his stubby body against the fence, crossed one foot over the other, and arranged his forearms along the top rail.

"Bravo, Miss Jasperton," he called.

Amilie smiled in response. So far, George had given her no firm reason to dislike or distrust him, but his manner of speaking to her was condescending and his smiles came closer to smirks.

Did Fitzhugh's dislike of George arise from the fact George would one day hold the title and Brompton Manor would be George's to command or was there something else?

Amilie dismounted, patted Shining Star's flank, and murmured words of praise to the mare. The groom took the reins from her hand and headed back to the stables with the horses.

George's eyes scoured Amilie from head-to-toe. His facial expression remained non-threatening during his close examination of her, but Amilie squirmed inwardly. She tugged at the bottom edge of the jacket of the borrowed riding habit whose separate pieces fit, except for the length of the jacket and the skirt. She tugged at the skirt.

"Permission to escort you back to the Manor house would please me." George tilted his head in her direction and tapped a riding crop against his leg.

Amilie hesitated. Her ride and her trotting lesson

served to refresh her spirit, but her melancholy still lingered to sober her mood. Unable to think of a gracious way to refuse, she gave her consent, performed a quick curtsy, and instructed herself to act pleasant.

"I believe the clouds decided to give up their game with the sun and are moving on," she said.

"So they are. But the radiance of your countenance outshines the sun on even a cloudless day."

Amilie covered her mouth to hide the grin forcing itself to her lips and bent down to pick a flower from the plantings lining the walkway. "My ride this morning went well," she said twirling the stem of the flower in her fingers. Amilie looked in George's direction. The expression on his face resembled the face of a lad who had participated in a footrace on a hot summer day—cherry red and filmed with perspiration. She lifted the flower to her nose. "The groom advanced me to a faster gait today."

George cleared his throat. "Your first time to trot a horse, Miss Jasperton?"

"Yes. But Shining Star is well trained and responsive to my commands. She is a joy to ride."

"And you, Miss Jasperton?"

Amilie giggled. "I suppose one might say I too am well trained. Perhaps not as easy to guide."

"Your father was vicar of a small parish I have been told."

"Yes."

"My father has fond memories of your mother. Your close resemblance to her was remarked on last evening."

"There is a portrait of my mother in Lady Brompton's dressing room."

"And you see yourself in the artist's depiction?"

"A similarity."

George peered at her. It was apparent he took the measure of things in the same manner as his mother, examining them intently to assess their worth.

"I have learned in addition to riding lessons, you will be afforded a dance master to instruct you in dance and proper etiquette," George said still peering at her.

"Yes."

"Lady Brompton has asked me to consent to partner you during your time with the dance master. I am honored to oblige, but only if you are in agreement."

"How kind of you to honor Lady Brompton's request. I fear I will require a great deal of assistance."

"If you learn dance steps with as much ease as you learn riding gaits, I have no fear of my being engaged for long."

"You flatter, sir."

George laughed a deep-throated chortle. "At times I find it necessary to flatter others, but not you, Miss Jasperton. I need only speak the truth where you are concerned."

A nagging concern about George's sincerity pulled Amilie's thoughts away from her upcoming dance lessons. She increased the length of her stride and the quickness of her steps. Perhaps his early acquaintance with George encouraged Mr. Fitzhugh to move fast.

Anyone with a modicum of pride, confronting George Mullerton's obsequious manner, would be desperate to escape.

With the hall door of her sitting room closed behind her, Amilie breathed a long sigh of relief. She could not find fault with George's overall demeanor toward her, but when she compared him to Fitzhugh, George's lack of height, his overall roundness, made an unflattering contrast to the defined, sculpted face and lean, muscular body of Mr. Fitzhugh. This contrast in their physical appearance made George outwardly unappealing. And lacking Fitzhugh's enthusiasm and energy, George seemed dull. But the manner in which George exhibited his superior status made her prickle with annoyance and wish to avoid him.

Amilie entered her bedchamber to change out of her riding habit and into an afternoon dress. An early morning note from Lady Brompton instructed her to come to her dressing room as soon as she had refreshed herself after her riding lesson.

Amilie stood in a spot from which she could study her mother's portrait hung on the wall in Lady Brompton's dressing room as she waited for her appearance.

"Oh Mama," she breathed aloud. "Would you be happy or sad I came here? Everything is more confusing to me, not less. I do not know if I should stay here or go." Sorrow pooled in Amilie's heart as she awaited an answer.

Before one came, Lady Brompton glided into the room. "Take a seat, my dear, and tell me why you look troubled today." She moved to stand next to Amilie and rested a hand on Amilie's shoulder.

Amilie squared her bowed shoulders, stilled her hands, and blurted out her anguish. "I have been here for some time and I have no answers to any of my questions."

"What questions do you have, Amilie?" The soft voice and even tone soothed the air in the room.

"Questions about why my mother was banished and why no attempt was made to reconcile with her. About Mr. Fitzhugh and his connection to Brompton Manor and why he displays his contempt for George."

Lady Brompton moved slowly around the perimeter of her dressing room; stopping to finger a vase, then picking up a porcelain and scrutinizing the figures, then brushing a piece of lint from her skirt. She stopped beneath the portrait of her daughter and stared up at it.

When she began to speak, her voice was barely above a whisper. "I gave birth to four children. Only your mother survived past the first two years. A measure of the strong will she possessed. When she was grown, she defied us and married your father, a lowly curate at the time, with no important family connections. By doing this, she relinquished all of the privileges and ignored all of the responsibilities her birth afforded her."

She pivoted to face Amilie. Tears streaked the powder on her cheeks.

Amilie rose to her feet and moved across the space to stand next to her. She reached out and took her hand in her own.

"What responsibility could my mother ignore? As a female, she could not inherit the Brompton title."

Lady Brompton closed her eyes. "My greatest sorrow in life was my inability to produce an heir who survived the nursery. Because of this, Brompton arranged for your mother, his only living child, to marry Mr. Mullerton, who is the heir presumptive and our current guest. By honoring our wishes, the honorary rank I hold would have passed to your mother upon the death of her father. Her strength of will, her intelligence, her love of this property would have served the title well. She defied our wishes and chose your father over duty."

"I see."

Amilie gazed at Lady Brompton for some time before she spoke again. "And you wish now for me to find favor with George, and he with me?"

"An arrangement is possible if you find you suit after you become acquainted. But, Brompton and I are wiser and a great deal older now. Your grandfather and I suited well. Many of my friends suited their mates less well and grew unhappy and bitter as the years passed."

Amilie lightly squeezed Lady Brompton's hand and leaned over to kiss her cheek.

"I hope I shall not disappoint you."

"I ask only a willing spirit and an honest heart. When you arrived, we found you a beautiful, sensible, and intelligent young lady and wanted you to have the opportunity to succeed me. Fulfilling my duties as the countess of Brompton, has given me great pleasure. But the decision is yours, Amilie."

"I thank you for your kind reflections on my character. The credit for any virtues I possess belongs to my mother and father. They taught me well."

"Yes." Lady Brompton lowered her eyelids concealing any emotion beneath the surface of her eyes.

"And Mr. Fitzhugh?"

"Colin Fitzhugh came to us through my cousin, who is a benefactor of a foundling hospital in London. Fitzhugh's birth parents are of Irish heritage, high-born and well-educated. That is all we were told. He has given us much joy."

"I see. And one day everything he knows and loves will be unavailable to him."

"True, one day my darling Brompton and I will be gone and Brompton Manor will be in the hands of the new earl, but Fitzhugh is capable of finding his way. He is spoiled because he is handsome and because his charming manner rivals Brompton's, but he was a serious student and carries a fine character and a level head."

Amilie nodded in agreement to her testament to Fitzhugh's character. Except for their highly improper encounter in the hall, his manner toward her was that of a true gentleman. His sensitivity and kindness had made her adjustment here easier.

After some thought, Amilie had concluded she was the one most at fault over this lapse. Because of her inexperience in these matters, she must have signaled to Fitzhugh she would welcome his intimacy.

Amilie shivered, her lips tingled with the memory of his lips pressed against hers. At first only a gentle brush, as though his lips were a feather, and then he pressed harder claiming her lips for his own. She laughed to shake off her wayward thoughts, best examined when she was alone, and got herself back to the present.

She rearranged the position of her ankles and smoothed the skirt of her dress. "George joined me at the riding ring today and accompanied me back to the house. He mentioned your request that he partner me during my dancing lessons. He asked my approval."

"And you gave your permission?"

"I did. I am eager to learn the steps of the dances. I should think dancing quite thrilling and await the instruction with enthusiasm. You were kind to arrange a partner for me. It will help me feel more secure."

Amilie's giggles merged with Lady Brompton's gay laughter.

"I grow fonder of you each day you are here, Amilie. But, there is a reason beyond providing an opportunity for you and George to become better acquainted to speed your dancing lessons along. I have invited many of our friends, with family members near your age, to the ball at Brompton Manor. I expect your dancing perfected so you might feel at ease. And dancing at the earlier assembly in the village will provide a place for you to practice the steps with different partners in public. By the time of the ball, you will feel comfortable in taking part."

"I am familiar with local assemblies. My parents allowed me to attend the last two held before . . . ," Amilie fought back a sudden wash of tears before she continued. "I was only allowed to watch the dancers from the sidelines, but this year I was to participate." Her lips quivered. She steadied them by holding her bottom lip with her teeth.

"Perhaps after meeting some of the young people in this country setting, where it is quieter, you will be eager to continue their acquaintance in London."

Amilie's feeling of warmth deserted her. "Perhaps."

"You looked exceptionally lovely last evening in your new dress."

"I'm glad you liked my surprise."

"A glorious surprise. I said nothing at the time so as not to embarrass you in front of the Mullertons. But Matilda Mullerton's favorable comments are limited to times when she is so overset with admiration she cannot silence her tongue. So, in regards to her reaction, you may count your dress a success."

"My one dinner dress was getting too much use. I purchased the silk fabric during my second trip to the village and Helaine cut and sewed the dress working into the late hours of the evening. A parlor maid, Molly, volunteered for the embroidery work. I stitched on the lace trim."

"My insisting Helaine and Molly work with the mantua-maker has been of great benefit to them. Perhaps one day they shall have their own shop."

Amilie nodded her head. "They both possess superior needle skills and a skilled eye to make the best use of a fabric. Since, I have learned, both read and cipher, I should think they would make a quick success of their own shop."

"They have a future if they should choose to leave us." Lady Brompton prepared to end the visit. "I believe we have come to an understanding today Amilie."

Amilie dipped a deep curtsy. "I harbored a foreboding that I would displease you and be banished like my mother before I could learn the reason for the estrangement. Thank you for taking the time to answer my questions. May I say something more before we part?"

"Of course."

"My mother's contentment and happiness with her way of life and with my father were evident every day."

A look of pain rippled across Lady Brompton's features. "I am glad. We loved her so," she murmured, keeping her eyes averted from Amilie.

"And the times she spoke to me of her childhood, she expressed only joy."

Lady Brompton clutched her chest and sprang to her feet. She struggled to speak. Clearing her throat and coughing. Her voice when she spoke was soft. "Tomorrow is a busy day for you. The dancing master and the mantua-maker are arriving . . . your riding lesson. Helaine will have your schedule." Lady Brompton pivoted and fled the dressing room before Amilie could rise to her feet.

Amilie's mood was high when she left the dressing room. She now had the answers she came here to find. She understood the suffering behind her grandparent's act and the reason for her mother's banishment. She now knew the reason for the pain that Fitzhugh concealed with his boisterous manner. She felt lighter as though a terrible weight were lifted from her. Her steps bounced. She was halfway to her apartments, counting the doorways and imagining what opening them might reveal. Someday she would take the time to look.

Fitzhugh came around the corner of an adjoining hallway. She slowed to a stop. She wanted to spin about and hurry off in the opposite direction, but he was speeding along at his usual pace with his head bowed. He closed the distance between them before she could flee.

"Miss Jasperton," he said looking up with a startled look on his face. He stepped back until he had his back flat against the wall.

Amilie gave a shaky laugh. "Mr. Fitzhugh, you resemble a ghost yourself today. You appear pale and unformed and lost." She felt her face heat at this feeble attempt to cover her discomfort at meeting this alluring man in a deserted hallway again.

Keeping his back against the wall, Fitzhugh tried to move past her. His hands were flattened against his thighs. No smile rippled his lips, fright showed in his eyes.

A painful twinge shot through Amilie's heart. Perhaps mere friendship between a gentleman and a lady was impossible after they exchanged a kiss. Perhaps he thought her too eager for his attentions, too forward in her behavior toward him, and was dismayed at coming face-to-face with her in the absence of others."

"Mr. Fitzhugh?"

Fitzhugh's body froze like an ice. His eyes searched wildly about the hall.

"Miss Jasperton?" His voice was strained.

Amilie clasped her hands together. She did not drop her eyes. "My apologies for enticing you into performing an improper act yesterday."

"Ah, Miss Jasperton. . . ." Fitzhugh stammered. His face was no longer ashen. His cheeks were a lovely shade of pink.

"I hope there will be no mention to others of my lack of decorum, Mr. Fitzhugh."

Fitzhugh drew himself up to his full height, skewered Amilie with his eyes, and cleared his throat. "Pray tell, Miss Jasperton, what would cause you to think I am less than a gentleman. A gentleman would never mention a lady's. . . ."

Amilie curtsied. She should not have spoken. She should have nodded to him and continued walking. She had implied she thought him less than a gentleman . . . a rake. "I think . . . I . . . ah," a wail escaped from somewhere deep inside. "I know not what I think." A shuddering breath followed her trembling words. She fled down the hall; away from his handsome face; away from the sight of his full lips; away from his bedeviling charms.

The odds of her finding George suitable while Fitzhugh resided in the same house were impossible. The only solution was for Fitzhugh or for her to depart Brompton Manor as soon as possible.

Amilie stopped pacing around the floor of her sitting room, pulled the bell chord, and settled into a chair to read from one of her books. The print blurred. She had to read the same paragraph several times.

She set the book aside when Helaine came through the door of her sitting room. "I rang because I am anxious to know if you have spoken with Mr. Fitzhugh."

"I wrote a note last evening and slipped the paper under his door. When he sought me out this morning, I hinted at his joining his friends in London by tomorrow."

"And his response."

"He agreed."

Amilie breathed a sigh of relief. "I encountered him in the hall moments ago and he acted in a most unusual manner. I fear my improper behavior ruined any chance of maintaining our friendship."

"Perhaps it has, miss."

Amilie strolled to one of the sitting room windows

and looked out. "I think I should like to walk to the village this afternoon. My last opportunity for a long walk, I expect. Tomorrow, in addition to my riding lesson, I face the mantua-maker and the dance master."

"I delight at the idea of another walk, miss. The mist has burned off and the day is cool and lovely."

Amilie faced into the room. Her will to remain at Brompton Manor strengthened now that the man who so disturbed her would be gone from sight and no longer haunt deserted hallways. "Then retrieve your bonnet and gloves Helaine and meet me in the entrance hall. I find my patience is strained by being cooped up in my room."

Stepping out the front door, the air warmed by the sun washed across their faces. Amilie pulled the brim of her bonnet forward to shield her face from the sun's strong rays. "I suppose I shall need parasols to keep the sun from ruining a pale, fashionable appearance."

"The mantua-maker will suggest accessories for each outfit. I imagine parasols and many other items. Her ladyship has a fur muff for winter."

"I plan to stop at the mercer's shop again today and ask him to show me his finest fabrics. Perhaps I will purchase some of the woolcloth he displayed yesterday."

"Your regular patronage of his shop is a compliment to him. If there is a fabric that takes your fancy he will supply it to the mantua-maker at her request."

"And I believe a stop for tea and an ice. A reward for

the long hours you spent sewing my dress. Her ladyship spoke highly of your and Molly's sewing, and Mrs. Mullerton was complimentary of the fabric."

The bell over the door of the mercer's shop jangled, as Amilie pushed the door open. The mercer finished a transaction with another customer. When he looked up and saw who had come in, his proprietor's welcome smile widened into a delighted grin. "Miss Jasperton, such an honor to have your visit to my humble establishment today."

"I wonder if you might show me some fabrics today, Mr. White. The mantua-maker is to arrive tomorrow."

"A pleasure to serve you in any way you desire, Miss Jasperton."

Today Mr. White did not clap for his assistant but pulled down several bolts of cloth and placed them on the counter himself. "The silks being woven in Spitalfields are as lovely as any of the French silks. The colors in these examples are flattered by you, Miss Jasperton."

The sight of the beautiful cloth pleased Amilie. All caution over expenditures was replaced by her anxiety over the number of dresses she would need for the upcoming social events she was to attend. She looked the fabrics over carefully. Two in particular appealed.

"This green silk with a beige stripe and the blue silk, shot through with gold threads will be perfect for the new ball gowns I will need. If you will set these two aside until the mantua-maker can order the correct length, I shall be appreciative.

"Delighted, Miss Jasperton. Your eye for quality is keen."

"And today, I plan to purchase some of the fine wool-cloth you showed me. Enough for a pelisse."

After the transaction was complete, Amilie opened her purse to pay.

"I will add this in when the order for the silk is complete, miss."

"But the purchase of the woolcloth is one I have chosen to make. I wish to pay for it with my personal funds."

"Of course, miss." The mercer took Amilie's coins. "If you find you would like some of the same woolcloth in a brighter color, I will be happy to show you samples of what is available and order the cloth from London.

"You are very accommodating, Mr. White."

Outside the shop, Amilie expressed her misgivings to Helaine. "Something has overcome my frugality, Helaine. I am exhibiting a scandalous disregard for thrift and an unchecked lust for fine fabrics."

"You have need of fine things, miss."

"The ability to buy things when I please, with no regard for the cost, is all new to me. I fear I will become a spendthrift."

"But miss, when you buy fabric, you keep the families of the weavers fed and in coals and when you use the services of the mantua-maker, you do the same for her."

Amilie laughed merrily and handed Helaine the package. "And when we enjoy our treat at the confectioner's shop, I will add to the comforts of the confectioner's family."

Helaine giggled. "You will, miss."

"My liberation from a need for thrift is heady.

The stroll to the confectioner's shop was undertaken without incident. Amilie entered the sweet-smelling shop in high spirits. The proprietor behind the counter looked up as she entered with Helaine. Surprise showed on his face as he looked from Helaine to Amilie.

Helaine spoke up informing him she now held the position of lady's maid to the earl of Brompton's granddaughter, Miss Jasperton.

The confectioner nodded and turned to Amilie. "I have fresh cakes and an excellent quality tea to offer my customers today, Miss Jasperton."

"I think tea and ices this afternoon. The perfume of baking in the air of your shop is enticing, but we shall confine ourselves today to cups of tea and pineapple ices."

Amilie took a seat at a table in the back corner. Helaine sat opposite, with her back to the door.

Amilie tucked a stray curl back beneath her bonnet. "I fear, in addition to becoming a spendthrift, I have developed a glutton's craving for frozen treats."

"Everything is new, miss. After a time, the temptations will diminish."

Amilie and Helaine were halfway through their ices

when the door flew open and a gentleman rushed through the opening.

"A few of your best cakes and a pot of tea," Fitzhugh's unmistakable voice called to the man behind the counter.

Amilie was elated. Fitzhugh had got over his reserve. He had returned to his normal show of exuberance.

He looked about, a delighted amusement shown in his eyes. He nodded to Amilie and Helaine.

"Perhaps you might join us, Mr. Fitzhugh," Amilie said when he neared their table.

"It will be my pleasure," he said and made a bow.

Taking a seat, he leaned in so he could whisper and not be overheard by anyone beyond the table. "I regret the need for intruding on your outing today, but I made a hasty decision. If I sat alone, the confectioner would think it odd people from the Manor were not sharing a table and there is no desire on my part to have him carry untrue tales about strained relations between those who reside at Brompton Manor."

Amilie did not believe a word of Fitzhugh's explanation but she did not wish to be rude to him in public which would cause tales to spread. "You are very careful of appearances, Mr. Fitzhugh."

Her ice melted as she stared at him. He was so close, sitting at this small table. She didn't wish him this close, it was too upsetting.

Their short conversation was stilted. Amilie rose from her seat, leaving half of her melting ice unfinished. She gave a cheery farewell to Fitzhugh to keep up appearances.

Fitzhugh scrambled to his feet, smearing cake frosting on his jacket. He wiped his lips, gathered his gloves, cleared his throat, and asked permission to join Amilie on her way home.

"We are afoot, Mr. Fitzhugh."

"As am I, Miss Jasperton." His words had a sorrowful note to them.

Amilie raised her head to look into his face. She wanted to reach out and offer him a comforting touch but she dared not.

"If I may be so bold," Helaine said sounding as stern as a school master. "We need to get on our way if you are to have time to change into proper clothes before dinner, miss."

"We shall walk at Mr. Fitzhugh's fast speed instead of my dawdling speed then," Amilie said forcing a laugh. "You may join us Mr. Fitzhugh and set the pace."

Helaine followed close behind Fitzhugh and Amilie. Once they were past the confines of the village and in the open countryside, Amilie began to speak to Fitzhugh in a soft voice. "I hope we are to remain friends, Mr. Fitzhugh. I understand you plan to leave Brompton Manor tomorrow."

"My request to leave before my scheduled date was denied, Miss Jasperton."

Amilie heard the sound of a loud gasp from behind her.

"Denied? By whom?"

"Lord Brompton. He believes George and I should be friends, and refuses to give up on the idea."

"Then a restoring of our friendship is in order."

"I am fortunate to have come upon you today, Miss Jasperton. I wished to offer my deepest apology for my odious behavior. I assure you, I desire nothing more than a friendship between us. I shall always regret having behaved toward you in such a detestable manner."

"Perhaps we both must take responsibility for the lapse of good manners. I do believe our recent sorrows may have caused a need within us to reach out and this resulted in each of us lowering our guard."

"I treasure your friendship and your level head, Miss Jasperton. You possess discernment uncommon to most."

They walked on, keeping to Fitzhugh's pace, until Amilie halted, removed her bonnet and cupped her hand at her ear. "Do you hear the bird singing, Mr. Fitzhugh? It is the song of the winter wren. I am delighted to hear him performing his complex and fife-like singing in this part of England. I often enjoyed their song where I was raised."

Fitzhugh eyed the juniper bushes growing in abundance along the edge of the road. "There, Miss Jasperton, do you see him flitting about in that bush, stopping to dine on one fat, blue juniper berry after another?"

"Yes. There," Amilie said pointing and laughing. "It is difficult to spot the winter wrens, they are so tiny but their song is so big. It is a marvel."

"Like you, Miss Jasperton."

Amilie looked up into the flushed face of the gentleman who constantly surprised her. Behind them Helaine made a loud clearing of her throat, breaking through the enchantment of the moment.

Fitzhugh adjusted his cravat and turned his head to look back in the direction of Helaine. "Have you seen the swans on the lake, Miss Jasperton?"

"I have. Upon my arrival two swans were gliding through the water of the lake, holding their long necks in their elegant manner as they swam along."

"I used to sit on the bank of the lake for hours watching them and skipping stones across the surface of the water."

They walked on in silence for a time.

Then Amilie spoke. "I believe providence sent me to the confectioner's shop today, Mr. Fitzhugh. My decision to visit the village today was made at the last minute."

"So it was not a desire to indulge your new found taste for ices?" Fitzhugh asked in a light, teasing voice.

"My desire for ices is on your conscience, Mr. Fitzhugh. It was at your insistence I sampled the first ice and now favor them."

Fitzhugh looked down the road. "I will return to London soon. I hope I may count on you to write me letters and keep me up-to-date on all of the events at Brompton Manor, Miss Jasperton."

"Your daily post will contain a note from me with all the news of the past day's events. I enjoy writing letters above all."

Amilie and Fitzhugh's friendly bantering caused

their pace to slow until Helaine prodded them onward with a reminder of the time. Fitzhugh sped up and Amilie kept up with him as they covered the remaining distance to the Manor house.

Chapter Fourteen

Two days later Brompton Manor hummed with activity. The clatter of iron wheels and the clop of the workhorses' hooves on the cobbled courtyard announced a steady stream of carts making deliveries. Inside the Manor house, maids and footmen bustled about with dusters and pails and scrub brushes.

Helaine was keeping a close eye on the manuta-maker as she fitted Amilie for her new outfits. Dress lengths, of the striped green and cream silk and the blue silk shot through with gold thread had been delivered and awaited cutting and sewing.

The blue fabric would be fashioned for Amilie's gown for the ball at Brompton Manor, the green fabric with the cream stripe would become her gown to wear to the assembly. Two riding habits were nearly complete. The orders for bonnets, gloves, reticules, parasols, and new underclothing had been posted to London. An urgent request for a pair of dancing slippers had been sent.

Each night, after the hubble-bubble of the day quieted, Amilie sat by the fire in her sitting room, opened the pages of her tattered copy of *The Pilgrim's Progress* and continued reading from the place she stopped the night before. The words of the story kept her thoughts from soaring to the boughs and her head from swelling to a size that would fit Prinny's coronet.

Her dancing lessons were progressing satisfactorily. She had mastered the steps to the quadrille—a dance touted by the dance master as all the rage in London. Tomorrow she would learn the steps to the waltz. The idea of swirling around a dance floor in a gentleman's arms excited her. The idea of being face-to-face with George damped her excitement.

George was gracious and patient as he partnered her at her lessons. He deserved only praise for taking part in her instruction. But she found him lacking in humor and curiosity, and his tendency for obsequious behavior became more pronounced the longer he was here.

Her posture had improved after the dance master's wife insisted she wear stays with a whalebone busk inserted into a placket down the center front. The inflexible busk served as a painful warning whenever her shoulders slumped.

She had learned to glide when she moved; her curtsy was more graceful. The etiquette of the dance, the dining room, and a proper demeanor when in the company of gentlemen were all part of her instruction—to prepare her for a future among society at the highest levels.

But after one arduous afternoon, when the dancing master made her walk from one side of the room to the other several times, expressing his unhappiness with her effort each time, she returned to her apartments tired and dejected, remarking to Helaine on how awkward she must have appeared when she had arrived at Brompton Manor.

"Your natural beauty, dignity, and grace evidenced themselves from the first, miss. Everyone below stairs commented. 'Tis the dancing master's duty to expect perfection from his students. He was hired for Mr. Fitzhugh."

"I do feel more confident of my manner, but learning how clumsy my walk and how bowed my back, I should think I resembled a foal trying to stand for the first time."

"At the assembly, miss, you will be the object of everyone's attention. They are curious to meet the earl of Brompton's granddaughter."

"I suppose my countenance and words will undergo the same close scrutiny they received from all of the widows and spinsters at home."

"Yes, miss."

Amilie removed the shoe from her left foot, undid her garters, and slipped the silk hose from each of her legs. "Perhaps hot water to soak my sore feet is in order? I am sure I heard a yelp from my left foot when I made a wrong turn and George Mullerton stomped on my toe."

Amilie held her exposed left foot up into the air. The big toe was red and swollen.

"Is Mr. George heavy-footed, miss?"

"He knows the correct steps to the dances and executes them with skill, but he lacks the natural athletic grace of Mr. Fitzhugh."

" 'Tis part of the troubles between 'em, miss."

"What troubles?" Amilie asked looking up from her examination of her toe.

"The reason Mr. Fitzhugh and Mr. George will never be friends."

"Because Mr. Fitzhugh is more graceful?"

"Because Mr. Fitzhugh has bested Mr. George at all of their games and contests since they were lads."

Amilie gazed at the coals in her fire grate. Some glowed red and others were reduced to ash. "But in the end, George will possess everything Mr. Fitzhugh covets," Amilie said. Her voice was muted, her gaze was directed somewhere beyond the walls of the room.

"Yes, miss." Helaine busied herself moving objects from place to place and opening and closing the curtains until she stopped, flopped down into a chair, and eyed Amilie.

"If I may, miss."

"My demands have wearied you, Helaine. You may go have a rest."

" 'Tis not a rest I need, miss."

"Then what?"

" 'Tis a sadness deep in my heart. I am fond of Mr. Fitzhugh. When he is unhappy, I am sad."

"I am fond of Mr. Fitzhugh too."

"I noticed, miss."

Amilie smiled a wry smile. "All of his energy and enthusiasm were quashed the moment the Mullertons arrived. And to add to his woe, I enticed him into lustful behavior. And when he tried to take your advice and leave for London, Lord Brompton denied him permission. I am sure he is feeling trapped and hapless."

"Pardon, miss, but I do not think it was your behavior caused Mr. Fitzhugh's lapse."

"Perhaps the blame is not mine alone, but being aware of my growing fondness for him, it was my place to keep a proper distance from him."

"Mr. Fitzhugh is difficult to keep a proper distance from, miss. He garners fondness from everyone he meets except for Mr. George."

"I wonder if he will attend the assembly and the ball."

"I am sure his lordship will insist. His absence would provide the gossips' tongues fodder."

"And after the Mullertons' visit, he will be free to leave Brompton Manor. Perhaps forever." Amilie heard the sadness in her voice. She would keep to her apartments away from the windows on the day of his departure. She would not watch him ride down the carriage lane, growing smaller and smaller until she could not see him anymore.

Helaine stood up. "I am off to find you hot water, miss."

As Helaine made her way to the door, Amilie saw her raise a hand to her cheek and heard her sniffs.

Helaine paused at the door, keeping her back to Amilie. Her words came out in a tremble. " 'Tis all changing so fast, miss."

Amilie knew Helaine's despair over Fitzhugh leaving was as deep as her own.

After Helaine left the room, Amilie moved to a chair by the window. " 'Tis all changing so fast," she muttered, parroting Helaine's lament. "I pray I am capable of making the right decisions in spite of the turmoil in my thoughts and in my heart."

Amilie entered her bedchamber and lay down on the bed. But sleep refused to come near and offer her respite.

Chapter Fifteen

Later that evening, after dinner had been enjoyed and the ladies had retired to the drawing room for their tea, the gentlemen were settled down to enjoy their stronger refreshments and one another's company.

The earl of Brompton tapped the table with the handle of a dinner knife he had retained.

Fitzhugh, George, and Mr. Mullerton lowered their snifters. Three sets of eyes settled on the earl of Brompton sitting in his place at the head of the table.

"Tomorrow additional guests will begin to arrive. After tonight, the time will be limited for the four of us to talk together. I will make a proposal this evening that will ensure the continued well-being of the Brompton holdings for the long future ahead."

Fitzhugh sat his glass down, placed his elbows on the

table, wove his fingers together to form a ledge, and rested his chin on his created structure.

George leaned back in his chair and crossed his arms across what promised to become a substantial stomach before long. Mr. Mullerton leaned his upper body closer to the Earl of Brompton and raised his eyebrows.

The earl of Brompton clutched the edge of the table with both hands, lifted his shoulders and took in a great lungful of air. "In the interest of time, I will state what I intend with no flourishes. I intend to place Fitzhugh in the position of steward of these estates and insist he retain this position after my passing."

With the exception of Lord Brompton, whose fierce glare at the others defied their quibbling, the other gentlemen at the table focused their attentions elsewhere. Fitzhugh drained the contents of his glass, George Mullerton studied the polished wood of the dining room table, and Mr. Mullerton stared at the far wall while nodding his head in rhythmic succession.

"Gentlemen?"

Mr. Mullerton stopped bobbing his head up and down and moistened his lips. "An impressive idea, I should think. But your proposal is premature. You appear to have recovered your health, and the current steward is quite able. However, when the time comes, I shall entertain some serious thought on the matter."

Fitzhugh poured brandy into his empty snifter and lifted the glass toward the earl of Brompton. The Mullertons' raised their glasses, to join the toast.

"To good health. To long life. To the earl of Brompton, may he enjoy many more years."

At the end of the toast, Fitzhugh sprang to his feet before the earl of Brompton rose from the table. The Mullertons' looked startled at the usurping of prerogative.

Fitzhugh covered his lips with his fingers. "I sincerely hope you will excuse me your Lordship. I fear for my dinner."

The earl's eyes skewered Fitzhugh.

Fitzhugh remained standing.

Then the earl of Brompton dropped his eyes, diffusing the strained atmosphere in the room, and gestured to Fitzhugh with a dismissive wave of the back of his hand. "You are excused, Fitzhugh. However, unless you are under the care of the physician, you will join in tomorrow's fishing party."

Fitzhugh bowed a deep bow. "Your lordship." He nodded to the Mullertons, and with strides longer than normal, with his right hand clamped over his mouth he hurried from the dining room.

"Well, gentlemen, time for us to join the ladies?" the earl of Brompton said, placing his palms flat on the top of the table and pushing himself upward.

Mr. Mullerton got to his feet all the while prattling about a recent encounter he had with one of his and the earl of Brompton's old school chums.

"Looked dissipated." Millerton said. "Beyond repair, I fear."

Lord Brompton concurred. "No doubt he is after his years of a profligate life."

"Started downward soon after he survived the duel with Lord Townsen," Millerton said.

"He severely wounded and disfigured Townsen in the process. Best friends for years, I imagine the disastrous foolishness weighed on him."

The three went single file through the dining room doors and headed toward the drawing room.

When she heard the footsteps of the gentlemen approaching the drawing room, Amilie went to the pianoforte and seated herself. Lord Brompton followed by Mr. Millerton, who was trailed by George, entered the drawing room. She expected to see Fitzhugh next. But he did not come in behind George.

George parted from the elder gentlemen and came to stand beside the pianoforte, making an offer to turn the music sheets.

She smiled her acceptance to his offer.

The crack of the earl of Brompton's knees, as he bent to lower himself into a chair, was loud enough to be heard across the room where the pianoforte sat. His sudden drop created the sound of a loud plop when he landed on the chair cushion. "I am delighted to see Amilie will be playing for us again this evening," he said loud enough to fill the room. Such a pleasure, this dear child. Speeded my recovery by weeks. Arrived here proficient at the keyboard and familiar with Mozart's compositions."

Amilie bowed her head. Her grandfather's complimentary words brought a smile to her lips. She wished she could have known him her entire life.

"Mozart, my dear child. Only Mozart," Lord Brompton called.

"I mean never to play any other composer's music when you are in the audience, Lord Brompton."

"You see," the earl of Brompton turned to address Mrs. Mullerton, "what an agreeable child our granddaughter is. Aims to please and carries a sweet countenance at all times."

George lounged at the side of the musical instrument, blocking her view beyond the candles illuminating her sheet music. She finished her first sonata, lifted her head, and smiled. "I hope you are as enamored of Mozart's music as his Lordship."

"Quite so. All music, played with skill, pleases me."

Amilie proceeded to play a piece she had practiced many times. Then another. Standing, at the conclusion of her third offering, she dipped her newly perfected curtsy.

George reached out to take her elbow and moved a step closer. "If I may, Miss Jasperton, a private conversation with you. Perhaps we might take seats near the windows."

As they walked from the pianoforte, Amilie noticed the self-satisfied smiles being exchanged between Lady Brompton and Mrs. Mullerton.

George took Amilie's elbow to assist her in sitting down. Then he drew up a small chair for himself. "You have a talent for the pianoforte Miss Jasperton. It is commendable. And the dancing master and his wife are doing an admirable job in refining your manner. Your dancing is graceful once you have the steps mastered. All in all I find you amenable to improving yourself. What of your education, Miss Jasperton? I don't expect you had much opportunity to study the classics. Nor should I find your lack of schooling a disqualification. If it is any comfort to you, I confess to finding women who have been educated, trying."

Amilie feared to speak her thoughts and struggled to remain seated.

George moved to the edge of his chair seat. "You were saying about your education, Miss Jasperton?"

Amilie squirmed for a few seconds before responding. She fought to keep her anger out of her voice. "I fear you shall be disappointed then, sir. My parents educated me quite thoroughly. I often quote from the classics, and my mathematical abilities are highly developed, sir."

George scooted back in his chair. Amilie bit her lip to keep from laughing at the look of consternation that flooded his face.

After sputtering for a few seconds, George got to his feet and offered his hand to Amilie. "Let us join the others, Miss Jasperton. I have kept you to myself too long. I am sure they are eagerly awaiting your presence so they might commend you on your performance."

When they reached the seated group, George saw Amilie to a chair near the others and wandered off.

Amilie listened to Lord Brompton and Mr. Mullerton as they discussed a lengthy speech given in the House of Lords the previous June. Mr. Mullerton paused to inform Amilie that holding a seat in the House of Commons he had heard only the briefest details of the speech and was delighted to hear first hand the speaker's stated reasons for and against imposing an additional tax on corn.

The earl of Brompton picked up the discussion again.

Lady Brompton turned to Mrs. Mullerton. "Really, if we must listen to such boring talk, I am ordering my workbasket brought. Would you like your workbasket brought also?"

"A wonderful idea. I am working an exquisite canvas and enjoy nothing more than keeping my hands occupied while listening to gentlemen converse over serious matters of state."

"You never enjoyed being idle for long," Lady Brompton said.

"I always say it is important to learn to handle one's time as though minutes had the value of shillings," Mrs. Mullerton replied.

"Why how wise. It never occurred to me to think of time as money." Lady Brompton motioned to a footman standing nearby. "Fetch Mrs. Mullerton's and my workbaskets."

The earl of Brompton got out of his chair. "Anyone for whist?"

"No cards tonight, Brompton. I sent a footman for our workbaskets."

Lady Brompton looked around the room. "Where is Fitzhugh, Brompton? He did not come in with you and still has not made his appearance."

"Excused himself, claimed a queasy stomach," the earl of Brompton said.

"His manner has been restrained the past few days. I hope his energies are not being affected by a renewal of the pain from his old battle wounds," Lady Brompton said.

"Perhaps he found his experience in America more trying than he lets on."

"Perhaps so. You must have a talk with him, Brompton, to see if you can discover what is making him so irritable and out of sorts."

"A good dinner and fine company were all I needed to recover fully. Perhaps good English fare and our expected company will aid Fitzhugh's recovery. He did mention the food in America was highly spiced."

Lady Brompton offered more tea all around and held out a dish of sugared nuts to Mr. Mullerton. The earl of Brompton hobbled across the room toward the writing desk.

Mr. Mullerton took a handful of the sugared nuts and chewed on them as he wandered about the room examining the paintings on the walls. Lady Brompton and Mrs. Mullerton plied their needles, while Amilie sipped her tea and observed the others.

The clock struck the quarter hour. The earl of Brompton crept up behind Mullerton and clapped him on the shoulder. "Billiards. Just the thing."

Mr. Mullerton jerked his head and covered his heart with his hand. "Quite a start you gave me, Brompton."

"Sorry. I find myself too stimulated to sit and write a letter. Felt up to a game of billiards for the first time in months."

"Happy to join you for a game. A fine way to top an evening. Perhaps George can be persuaded to join us," he said and loped off toward his son who was making a close examination of items across the room.

"Sir?"

"Inviting you to join Brompton and me in a game of billiards."

The gentleman excused themselves from the presence of the ladies. George waved his eyebrows up and down at Amilie. "Tomorrow the waltz, Miss Jasperton."

The thought would keep her awake all night. "And the canter," she said. "Difficult tests of my physical aptitude to look forward to."

"Tests you are sure to pass with ease."

With a chilling, possessive, leering smile at her, George followed Lord Brompton and his father from the drawing room.

Amilie kept her seat and her own counsel for several minutes. George's manner made her wary of him. She suspected George hid a despotic personality behind his outward show of deference toward her. She hoped he did not find she suited.

Chapter Sixteen

After he left the dining room, Fitzhugh got to his apartments and sprawled into a chair. He covered his face with his hands. The pain in his heart was more intense than the pain he had felt when the bullet slammed into his leg. He could not continue going forward with a broken heart any more than he could have moved forward with the bullet in his calf. In both instances, he could only watch in agony from behind the lines, incapable of fighting on.

Jumping to his feet, he entered his bedchamber and packed a small bag. He would go tonight. He could no longer abide watching Amilie and George together. Despite the eternal gratitude he had to the earl of Brompton for taking him in and as much as he loved this estate, he would never accept the position of land steward and be subject to the Mullertons' dictates one day.

His love of Brompton Manor, his debt to his guardians, and his concerns for the well-being of the tenants and the villagers could not overcome the loathing he had for George Mullerton. He would rather starve in the streets of London.

He closed the small bag and strode from his sitting room, escaping the confining walls and the stuffy air inside the house would be a start. Gaining the entrance hall, he nodded to the night porter and sailed out the entrance door. Stumbling in the dark, he headed toward the lake.

Sitting down on the grassy bank, he brought his knees to his chest, wrapped his arms around his legs, and laid his face atop his knees. The sound of his sobs blended with the chirping of the crickets and the croaking of the frogs.

For all of his years at Brompton Manor, he knew the day the title passed, his connection to the estate would be severed too. But, now his ineligibility to inherit also made him ineligible for the woman who dominated his waking thoughts and appeared in his nighttime dreams.

The granddaughter of the earl of Brompton belonged here—destined to become the countess of Brompton when George took the title following his father's tenure. Respect for Lord and Lady Brompton prevented him from interfering with their wish to see Amilie married to a future heir. And for the first time in all of the years they had known one another, George Mullerton would prevail.

A mental picture of himself strolling through the back

streets of London, wearing shabby clothes, his cheeks sunken, his teeth missing, flashed into his mind. Fitzhugh chuckled and lifted his head. The clouds had parted. Moonlight colored the water of the lake. The air was soft and a light breeze dried the moisture on his cheeks.

A trust fund had been settled on him the moment he became the earl of Brompton's ward. The fund provided him enough income to keep him in food, reasonably housed, and clad in decent clothing. Loitering about the streets of London with a tin cup in his hand or pushing a vendor's cart would not be his fate.

Wiping his eyes and giving his nose a good blowing, Fitzhugh cupped a hand and dipped it into the water of the lake. He splashed a handful of the cool water over his face, pulled his shirttail from his breeches, and dried his face.

Getting to his feet, he strolled along the path that ran around the edge of the lake. An owl sounded in the distance. The frogs and crickets kept up their racket. Life went on. So would he.

He would not allow George's presence to force him into leaving early. He would stay at Brompton Manor and suffer the pain. But as soon as he eyed the rear of the Mullertons' traveling carriage, he would depart for London and never look back. How he would cope with seeing Amilie each day and not showing his true feelings for her, he could not fathom, but he must and he would.

Amilie lay in her bed wishing she could sleep but knowing she had too much to sort out before she allowed herself to drift off. Perhaps a visit to the squire and his family would be helpful? The distance from Brompton Manor would allow her to gain perspective on the advantages offered to her here.

As countess of Brompton, it would be easier to fulfill a duty to aid the poor, but was that enough reason to dismiss her objections to George?

She needed to get away before losing her ability to leave the promise of financial ease and the luxury trappings of the most privileged in society. And she needed to distance herself from Colin Fitzhugh. He clouded her judgment. His appeal was stronger than the elegance of the estate surroundings, the opportunities for riding, the attentive servants, dancing parties, and the financial means to purchase all the beautiful fabrics she could want. He filled her heart.

She yearned for a marriage filled with love and laughter and respect. The kind of marriage her parents enjoyed. Her mother had married the man she loved and given up all of this for him. She could too. Except the man she loved did not love her.

And George Mullerton did not suit. If he made an offer, she would refuse.

Giving up on sleep, Amilie secured her shawl around her shoulders and moved to sit in a chair by the banked fire in her sitting room. Thinking she might read, she lighted several candles and took up her book, but the words blurred into a meaningless jumble.

Taking the candleholder with her, she sat down at her writing desk and began a note.

Dear Mr. Fitzhugh,
I fear I am hopelessly in love with you. My lack of restraint has caused our friendship to suffer. Forgive my boldness in informing you of this.

Sincerely,
Amilie Jasperton

She folded her note and pulled her shawl tighter about her shoulders. Opening the door of her sitting room, she looked up and down the hall. Seeing no one about, she stepped out into the hall and closed her door with a soft click.

She paused in front of Fitzhugh's door. A light shone from beneath his door. He must be awake. But she had dared to come this far and her mission required only seconds more to complete. She bent down and pushed the note through the slit between the bottom of the door and the floor. She teetered, fell forward, banged her forehead against the door, and ended on her knees. Her dismay only increased when the door in front of her nose opened a crack and Fitzhugh's face appeared in the opening. Her heart flipped like an acrobat; her breath deserted her.

"Miss Jasperton, what are you doing?"

"Delivering a note, Mr. Fitzhugh." Amilie gripped both sides of the doorframe and pulled herself to her feet. "I thought it important."

"I hope the message is of such importance and urgency it makes it worth the scandal that would arise if someone saw you outside my door this time of the night clothed in your nightrail," he said in a stage whisper. "Now hurry along to your apartments before the ghost who haunts these halls appears. And don't dawdle."

A real ghost!

Amilie's hand covered her gaping mouth. Fitzhugh's admonishment ended her paralysis. She sped back to the safety of her apartments.

After Amilie disappeared, Fitzhugh picked up her note, unfolded the paper and read the words.

Lady Brompton sent a summons for Amilie to appear in her dressing room before her riding lesson.

When Amilie arrived, Lady Brompton was already seated and began to state the purpose for her request for Amilie's appearance the moment she was seated.

"Amilie dear," she said. Her eyes were full of warmth today. "I meant to go through my guest list with you before now, but all of your time is taken by your lessons and your fittings. I wanted to tell you I am having a list drawn containing the names, titles, and small personal details about each of the expected guests. Go over the information whenever you have a few spare moments. If you have questions, send a note. I will respond. Now you are free to go on with your day."

Amilie nodded, kissed Lady Brompton's cheek, and hurried off to her riding lesson.

When the riding ring was visible, she saw George was mounted and waiting to accompany her. Her heart quivered with irritation.

Amilie spoke to the groom, requesting a new trail for today. She did not wish her pleasant memories of the previous trials she had ridden spoiled by retracing them with George.

George looked down at her from his perch atop his horse. "Perhaps I might suggest one, Miss Jasperton. Which trails have you undertaken previously?"

Amilie looked to the groom who gave George the information, then nodded her agreement when George named his choice of unexplored trails.

She mounted. George rode next to her.

"You appear less than cheery this morning, Miss Jasperton."

"My sleep last night was fitful."

"Perhaps dinner was too rich and our conversation too stimulating to allow you a proper rest."

"Perhaps."

"And I should think the full schedule you have been forced to undertake to get you prepared has been taxing for you."

Amilie ignored the invitation to remark on her schedule and changed the direction of the conversation. "Shining Star is the best horse ever. I should hate to have to leave her."

George Mullerton cleared his throat and swept his hand before him in a grand gesture. "Everything at Brompton Manor is the best that is available."

"What allows you your greatest pleasure here, Mr. Mullerton?"

"The hunting at Brompton Manor is unrivaled in all of England."

"I am very fond of birds and animals. The deer are beautiful creatures. They freeze in place, at the edge of the tree line, poised to flee at the first indication of danger."

"And delicious. A roasted haunch of Brompton Manor venison is a treat you have yet to experience."

Amilie called to the groom. "A return to the riding ring is in order."

The groom nodded to acknowledge her demand. As soon as the path widened enough for the horses to swing around, he reversed their direction.

"I am sorry to curtail our ride, but my loss of sleep has caused my strength to flag."

"You are doing extremely well. The strain to acquire the polish you need to become presentable to society in such a short amount of time has burdened you."

Amilie's stomach churned, layers of anger worked upward smothering her voice.

"Miss Jasperton?"

Amilie managed a wavering smile and called to the groom to go faster.

Back at the riding ring, George doffed his hat. "My apology for upsetting you Miss Jasperton. I hope to make amends during your dance lesson today."

Amilie nodded and followed the groom into the riding ring. George Mullerton was an insufferable bore, so arrogant, so impressed by his place in society. Did he possess any redeemable qualities that would mitigate his undesirable personality traits? From her earliest days of understanding, her father admonished her to look for the best in people, and not dwell on their failings. But some people managed to disguise any of their good qualities so thoroughly it made the task difficult. George Mullerton was difficult.

"Miss, time for your dance lesson," Helaine stood next to Amilie's bed, shaking Amilie's shoulder and speaking in a loud voice.

Amilie's awareness swam up through the depths of her sleep. "I am far too tired, Helaine. Please inform the dance master I will not present myself for instruction today."

"Yes, miss." Helaine placed a light blanket over Amilie and pulled the bedchamber curtains closed. "Sleep until 'tis time to dress for dinner. The mantua-maker is busy completing the outfits already cut and fitted and the dance master's time here is extended until after the ball. Her ladyship decided to make his instruction available to any of her young guests who desire to learn to waltz."

Amilie muttered her acknowledgement of Helaine's words, placed the palms of her hands together, and tucked them beneath her head. The lids of her eyes fluttered then closed.

* * *

Fitzhugh entered the drawing room before dinner, appearing on time with an elaborately tied cravat, a restored enthusiasm, and his familiar energetic stride. He formally acknowledged those already present, leaving Amilie for last and giving her only a brief glance and a curt nod before turning away.

"A wonderful day for fishing," the earl of Brompton boomed out. "Fitzhugh won the day. Caught more browns then the rest of us combined. Reeled in an eight-pounder, he did. Cook is instructed to have the champion fish prepared and included on the table for our enjoyment tonight. Nothing like fresh fish retrieved from the splendid waters of my very own streams."

Lady Brompton rose, exhorted the others to rise, and form the procession.

Amilie took George's extended arm. Fitzhugh trailed behind.

"Miss Jasperton," George said. "I must express my excessive disappointment when I learned you would be absent from your dance lesson this afternoon. I left the pleasure of the fishing party early to return in time to aid you in your attempts to learn the waltz."

"My apologies, Mr. Mullerton. Tomorrow will be time enough."

"Sorely disappointed. I should hate to have my enjoyment of the assembly ruined by foregoing the opportunity to partner you for your first public waltz because you have failed to master the steps."

Fitzhugh's harrumph from behind gave Amilie a start. George swiveled his neck. Amilie saw he was staring swords at Fitzhugh.

"I hear you have are a master of the waltz, Mullerton," Fitzhugh offered.

"Quite so." George returned his attention to Amilie and preened.

At the table, Amilie was seated beside George who used the time to relate stories to her about previous dances he had attended, the partners he had favored, and the compliments they had given him. Amilie's ability to enjoy the splendid array of dishes offered was diminished by being forced to listen to George's self-aggrandizing conversation and the sight of Fitzhugh seated across the table. She would speak with Lady Brompton and request that after tonight Fitzhugh be seated on the same side of the table she was seated on with a minimum of two chairs between them.

Soon after the gentlemen joined them in the drawing room, Amilie requested permission to be excused. Amilie tried to not fidget as she waited for the delayed response to the request. She saw concern in Lady Brompton's eyes as she studied her for what seemed an endless time.

"You may be excused, dear child. Rest as much as you can before our other guests begin to arrive. The list I promised should be in your apartments."

"Thank you, I will take some time to go over the list before I fall sleep."

"My sister, my niece, and my grandniece are expected tomorrow. They are arriving early to attend the assembly and pay a longer visit then our other expected guests. I have listed their names at the top. I believe you will find my grandniece, Jane, a delightful companion."

Amilie made her curtsies, left the company and started up the stairs. Perhaps her flagging energy came not from too much activity, but from the uneasiness and confusion that grew more pronounced after each encounter with George. He was insufferable. Even her beloved father's limitless patience would have been sorely tested by George.

In her room, Amilie found the list atop the table beside a wing chair. She picked it up and riffled through the five pages covered with writing. The lines were closely spaced. Each sheet of paper was covered on both sides. Despite the overpowering weariness she felt, she sat down in a chair, covered a yawn and studied the first name on the list.

"Catherine Hornby, the Viscountess deVale," she said aloud. She had heard this name before. The memory of a lady who arrived at the vicarage one day in a shiny carriage pulled by a matched pair of white horses, a lady who wore a silky dress and with plumes adorning her bonnet, flooded into Amilie's mind. Her mother introduced her to Amilie as Lady deVale and when the visit ended, her mother explained Lady de-Vale was her aunt and a great aunt to Amilie. The occasion of the visit provided Amilie the only memory she had of seeing her mother in tears.

Chapter Seventeen

The bed, where Amilie took shelter from the thundering storm of her emotions, offered little rest even though she soon fell into an exhausted sleep. She woke to find only a weak light showing around the edges of her windows. A deep sense of dismay nagged at her and refused her any more sleep. She rang for Helaine.

"Miss?" a breathless Helaine said as she rushed into Amilie's bedchamber with Amilie's morning cup of chocolate. Setting the cup down on the nightstand, Helaine straightened her mobcap and wiped a crumb from her lip.

"I rang you during your breakfast time, because it is urgent to get a note to the stables. I wish to inform the groom I will ride an hour earlier today."

"Yes, miss."

"And after the message is delivered, you may finish

your breakfast. I will complete my toilette this morning and proceed to the riding ring at the earlier time on my own."

"Yes, miss."

After Helaine departed, Amilie sipped at her chocolate. It was a brilliant idea. By moving up the hour for her riding lesson, she eliminated the possibility of George accompanying her on her ride today. The grotto, mentioned at the dinner table last evening, was her destination, and she had no desire to entertain George while she explored the cave, like structure Fitzhugh had described.

"I doubt George would use the opportunity to exhibit any redeemable qualities, anyway," she muttered as she slipped out of bed, washed her face and neck, arranged her hair, and donned her riding habit.

Amilie's steps were buoyant as she made her way along the now familiar path to the riding ring. A gush of air escaped from the depths of her lungs when she saw there was only the groom and two horses awaiting her arrival.

"I wish to explore the grotto, today," she instructed as she stepped onto the mounting block."

"It is not far, miss. A nice, gentle ride."

The silent journey, in the early hours of the morning, with a slight breeze carrying a musty scent from the floor of the woodlands, calmed her spirit. A doe and her fawn appeared on a rise in the near distance. They stood frozen as though in a painting until the crack of a tree limb sounded and they fled.

Amilie enjoyed roast venison, when the meat was offered at table, she had enjoyed her portion of the fish
Fitzhugh had caught and Cook prepared for last evening's dinner. But she did not want to look into the eyes
of the deer or breathe along with the moving gills of the
fish or stroke the feathers of the fowl before their flesh
became sustenance.

George made clear he found great pleasure in chas-
ing and felling meat to supply the table. Did his enjoyment in watching animals suffer extend to humans?
Had his remark about her lacking in the refinement required in the upper levels of society been made inten-
tionally to hurt her? Fitzhugh never said cruel things to
her or implied she was less than acceptable because of
the limited opportunities of her upbringing.

Amilie stilled her troubling thoughts by concentrating on the beauty of the trail. The path took them
through a wooded area that opened to a large clearing.
She moved her head from side to side to take in the
vista spread out before her. To her right a stream flowed
through an arched stone outlet. A flat bridge was sup-
ported by the arch. The front of a structure that had
been built against a hill had a cave-like entrance in its
center. The fronts of two rotundas flanked either side.

"The grotto, miss." The groom helped Amilie dismount and took Shining Star's reins.

Amilie walked across the bridge and peeked into the
grotto from the entrance. She caught her breath. Peering back at her, from the rear of the center structure,
was a marble statue of a figure resembling depictions

she had seen of the god, Neptune. Beneath the statue, water splashed from one basin into another then into another before disappearing beneath the floor. She stepped inside. The air carried the same properties as the air in the ice house, cool and still with a slight dampness. But here, the sound of water spilling from one basin into another and the absence of Fitzhugh's fitful energy relaxed her. Amilie passed through a smaller opening into the rotunda on her right. Another marble statue filled a niche in the far wall. The walls, covered with shells and sunlight, penetrated the area through a small square opening.

"Achoo."

Someone was in the main chamber.

The groom was too far away to hear her if she screamed.

Her heart faltered, her knees quivered, prickles of fear ran along her spine. She wanted flee like the dear when they caught the sound of danger. She grasped the bottom sill of the square opening. Perhaps she could pull herself up, squeeze through the narrow slot, and escape.

"Miss Jasperton?"

Amilie instantly recognized Fitzhugh's voice and eased her grip on the stone at the bottom of the opening. Her fear turned to anger. Wiping her hands down the side of her dress, she whirled about to face him.

"The sound of your sneeze frightened me." Amilie said in a crisp, accusatory tone.

"My apologies, I thought to find you in the main chamber and failed to call out to alert you to my presence."

"What are you doing here? Did you follow me, thinking I would forget myself again?" Amilie looked away from the swell of his lips and the sudden longing in his eyes. "If so, you have wasted your time because I will not."

Fitzhugh dipped a small bow. His shoulders were shaking. "Your message about moving your lesson ahead by an hour arrived at the stables as I was preparing to ride. I thought to use the opportunity to speak to you privately, without raising questions in the minds of others. It seemed a good idea to me when I thought of it."

"I think we have nothing left to discuss. My note explained my failings and my regrets." Amilie fought to keep her sorrow from her voice.

"I wanted to tell you, I believe you have mistaken your feelings for me, Miss Jasperton. Loneliness creates a longing within us that we seek to fill. My presence here gave you someone to focus on to fill the empty space created by your recent loss."

"I see."

Fitzhugh took a step forward, and then another and then, he came close enough to reach out and brush back the tendril of hair that had escaped from the neat bun she had fashioned. He wet his finger and wiped a smudge from her nose. "Your company has filled my loneliness too." Fitzhugh dropped his hands and stepped back. "Friends, Miss Jasperton?"

"Friends, Mr. Fitzhugh." Amilie managed a weak smile. To experience his lips on hers once more was what she truly longed for, but it was her friendship to ease his loneliness in the absence of others that he desired, not her love.

Amilie felt her heart crack, but by making a great effort she held onto her dignity.

Emerging from the grotto, and blinking in the bright light, Amilie thought herself in full control of her emotions again. The murkiness and serene atmosphere in the grotto lowered her resistance.

She requested Fitzhugh partner her for the first set at the assembly. "I should feel confident with you as my partner. You will not laugh if I stumble or become confused about the steps."

"I promise you my best efforts," Fitzhugh said managing a laugh. "It is an unfair competition between George and me on the dance floor. I am a much better dancer then he."

"Good, Mr. Fitzhugh. Good. It will be a delight."

Fitzhugh gave Amilie a long, lingering look. His face sobered. He clamped his lips together for a time. Then he spoke. "You need to face George square on, Miss Jasperton."

"I suppose I must, Mr. Fitzhugh. I am glad you sought this opportunity to mend our friendship and offer your advice."

Fitzhugh touched the brim of his hat and dipped a bow.

"Who is represented by the statue in the rotunda in which you found me, Mr. Fitzhugh?"

"Minerva, the Roman goddess of wisdom."

"And is there a statue in the opposite rotunda?"

"Yes. Venus. The Roman goddess of love."

Amilie felt a rush of heat rise into her cheeks. She waved her hand and called good day over her shoulder as she scrambled up the hill to the spot where Shining Star was waiting.

Chapter Eighteen

When the carriage with the grandniece, niece, and sister of Lady Brompton turned into Brompton Manor's carriage lane, Amilie was seated at her writing desk composing a note to one of the widow ladies who lived in her home village.

Alerted by the sound of carriage wheels in the courtyard, she peeked out her window to make an assessment of the expected arrivals.

Their clothing and the number of portmanteaus strapped to the rear of the private traveling carriage attested to the financial well-being of the passengers.

"I must not take instant offense to Miss Jane Owens . . ." Amilie muttered. ". . . because she arrived in a manner befitting a diamond of the first water does not speak of her character."

She turned from the window. *If father knew I am*

covetous of others, he would frown at me to show his displeasure.

After thinking for a while, she rang for Helaine.

"Yes, miss?" Helaine said when she entered the sitting room.

"I wish the manutua-maker to set aside my riding habits and my ball gowns for a time and freshen my green muslin day dress. I plan to wear the dress this afternoon and it is too plain for the grand occasion of being introduced to the arriving guests. A bit of lace would give it an added flair."

"Right away, miss. There are many boxes filled with lovely trim in the sewing room." Helaine took Amilie's green muslin dress from the wardrobe and hurried off with it draped over her arm.

As the dismals settled over her spirit, Amilie curled up in a wing chair. Keeping oneself fashionable required a shallow understanding of the worthiness of an endeavor. Worrying about the surface impression one made on others was a vanity and wasteful of both time and money. But, she did not want Jane Owens to dismiss her on first sight.

With a sigh breathy enough to extinguish a candle, Amilie got to her feet and returned to the window.

Living amidst the abundance of Brompton Manor confused her sensibilities. Or perhaps George's scornful remarks had penetrated deeper and hurt more than she should have allowed.

She busied herself with aimless tasks and watched

the hands of the clock tick away the minutes as her anxiety increased with each click of the minute hand.

An hour and a half later, Helaine returned to the sitting room and held up the green dress for Amilie's inspection. Delicate ecru lace encircled the neckline; a woven, yellow trim edged the sleeves and hem and encircled the empire waistline.

"How much nicer my dress looks with these additions."

"And I found a matching green ribbon for your hair, and miss, I brought along some seed pearls to secure to the hair ribbon."

"I will look very grand in my refashioned dress with a green ribbon, spiked with pearls, winding through my hair."

"Yes, miss."

Helaine finished enhancing the ribbon with the seed pearls and laid it atop Amilie's dressing table then went to fetch Amilie's lunch and some warm wash water. When she returned, Helaine handed Amilie a note from Lady Brompton instructing Amilie to appear in the yellow drawing room at three o'clock.

"Then I have enough time for a nap before I am to meet my aunts and my cousin." Amilie picked up the orange brought with her lunch tray, removed the peel and broke the fruit into individual sections.

Helaine knelt down to tend the fire grate.

"Are you familiar with Miss Owens, Helaine?"

"She comes each year with Lady deVale, her grandmother, and some years she comes a second time with her mother."

"Her mother has no title?"

"No, miss. I believe she married the second son of a viscount."

"Is Miss Owens pleasant?"

"Yes, miss. I believe she is." Helaine pulled the curtains across the windows, blocking out the afternoon sun. "I will return in time to help you dress for the afternoon, miss."

Rested from her nap, dressed, and freshly coifed, the seed pearls peeking out from between the curls atop her head, Amilie took Helaine's maps from a drawer in her writing desk. The location of the yellow drawing room still remained a mystery after some minutes of looking.

"The ground floor, miss."

Amilie positioned the ground floor map to the correct orientation and traced the route from the grand staircase to the room labeled yellow. "I am off, Helaine. Confident now of my direction."

"You look lovely, miss," Helaine said as Amilie squared her shoulders and took a deep breath.

Gaining the ground floor, Amilie turned to the left of the grand staircase, entered a long hall, and counted doors. Three doors on the right, and then the first door on the left should be the room she wanted.

When she entered the doorway, the footman on duty clicked his heels together and announced her.

Five pairs of eyes stared at her. Amilie's knees wavered. To give herself confidence, she formed her lips into the same smile she offered her father's parishioners when entering the church on a day of worship. A genuine and warm smile she had been told. And it was sincere. She hoped the smile on her face today would be perceived as genuine and warm too.

Lady Brompton rose to greet her, made introductions, and beamed. Mrs. Mullerton reached out and patted Amilie's arm.

"Amilie, Jane promised to tell you all about London. She made her come-out during last year's Season, and was a huge success," Lady Brompton said as she and Amilie sat down.

Jane giggled. "Not so great a success, Miss Jasperton, as to receive an offer, but I never sat out a dance, if that is a measure of success."

Amilie found Jane Owens face open and cheerful and her demeanor friendly. She showed no traces of conceit.

"I love nothing more than to relate all of the current London *on dit*. I hope you enjoy listening to gossip, Miss Jasperton."

"I am happy to listen, although I will not know any of the subjects of the gossip."

"Then we shall have a walk about the gardens, and I shall tell you all about the first ball I attended and describe everything in detail. There was quite an exciting incident. I think it will shock you."

"Jane. You are not to shock Amilie with lurid tales of the misdeeds of others. And wait until after tea to have your walk together. Cook has prepared special treats."

"Delightful." Jane clapped her hands together. "I suspect Cook made her delicious macaroons, and I will eat too many biscuits and spoil my dinner." Jane looked at Lady Brompton from the corner of her eye. "I promise I shall curb my tongue," she said and laughed gaily.

Amilie was drawn into Jane Owens web of delight and found nothing about her to dislike or to make her cautious in her approach. Miss Owens was not the person who hid their fine qualities and forced one to go in search of them.

Cups of tea were passed around, biscuits chosen and remarked on, and the girls' bonnets and gloves sent for. The rest of the conversation had centered on the guests' journey to Brompton Manor. Comments were offered comparing this trip to those made before.

To Amilie, any upset or disaster they had encountered seemed insufficient to cause a person much distress. But she refrained from mentioning the harrowing details of her own trip to Brompton Manor or the use of a crowded public coach, a lopsided dray, and the walk it took to get her to the door.

The biscuit plate empty and their second cups of tea finished, Lady Brompton gestured to Amilie and Jane. "Now, off with the two of you. The flowerbeds surrounding the lake are replanted with chrysanthemums and asters in preparation for our picnic outing. Perhaps you would care to view them."

"The lake is a great destination, and I am desirous of a long walk," Jane said leaping to her feet. "That is, unless Miss Jasperton would choose otherwise."

"I love to walk and distance is no hindrance to my enjoyment, Miss Owens."

Once again, Jane Owens clapped her hands and laughed a trilling laugh. "We shall be bosom-friends, Miss Jasperton. All of my Town acquaintances wrinkle their noses and go about in a pout when I suggest we travel even the shortest of distances on foot."

Laughing together, the two young ladies entered the reception hall and donned their bonnets and gloves.

As they headed toward the lake, Jane chattered away. She described the lovely parks in London, the shops that carried goods from around the world, the availability of many different choices for one's entertainment. Then she spoke of the shock she caused when she refused an offer of being driven about in a wheeled conveyance and chose instead to walk in the London parks accompanied by a footman.

She turned to Amilie. "I imagine it a great adventure, being the daughter of a vicar. Everyone would recognize you and visit with you and be kind to you. Do call me Jane, Miss Jasperton. We will have such fun walking in the parks together."

"And call me Amilie, Miss . . . Jane."

"Oh, this is more than I ever expected. All the way here, I sat in dread of finding you dour and a stickler for proper behavior."

"And I dreaded that you would find me dull and peevish," Amilie said and laughed.

"Well, I am delighted you are none of those things."

Jane leaned closer to Amilie's ear. "I am up in the boughs about seeing George Mullerton again." She looped her arm through Amilie's.

Amilie's right foot hung in suspension for a moment before she managed to place it on the ground and lift her other foot.

"Truly?"

"He attended me at every ball last Season. Favoring me with the waltz on three occasions and the supper dance twice."

"I am learning the waltz."

"The waltz is the most exhilarating of dances. My favorite. It is so stimulating to be held by a gentleman and whirled about the floor."

"George informed me he favors the waltz and desires a skilled partner to accompany him. You must be an accomplished dancer if George partnered you on so many occasions."

Jane stopped walking and turned to face Amilie. The expression on her face was solemn. "I find George Mullerton a handsome and exceedingly pleasant gentleman, but there is not even the merest suggestion of any agreement between us. I did not mean to overstep, if you favor him, Miss Jasperton."

"Do not concern yourself over this matter, Jane. George has been kind and generous helping me learn the dance steps, but I am not distressed in the least to learn you find him appealing."

"George offers the highest degree of thoughtfulness to others," Jane said as they continued to the lake.

Amilie felt a burden lifting from her shoulders. George would be flattered and fawned over by Miss Owens and she could concentrate her energy on finding ways to avoid him.

"Look at the water of the lake, Amilie. The breeze is making ripples all across the width and the sun is painting the ripples with streaks of gold."

"When I first arrived here, I stood on the bridge for some time and took in the beauty of this lake. The waters offer a soothing quality and an unfathomable depth that attracts speculation. The lake and the sun have combined their efforts to put on their finest display today in honor of your visit, Jane."

"You have a wonderful and fanciful imagination, Amilie. I am very fond of delightful thoughts. When I was a child, I pretended elves and fairies lived in sparkling cities of gold beneath these waters."

"I should be delighted to imagine the same."

Jane burst into peels of laughter.

Amilie pointed toward the colorful beds of flowers edging the lake. "The new plantings add a nice burst of yellow and rust to the landscape."

"Colorful roof tiles for our underwater friends perhaps."

Amilie giggled at Jane's remark.

"There will be small boats on the lake on the day of the picnic." Jane said. "Every year the earl of Brompton rows the countess of Brompton to the middle of the lake, stands up in the bow while she grips the sides of the boat, and sings her a love song."

Amilie stared at the water. "I have noticed their great fondness for one another."

"I hope Lord Brompton's illness does not prevent him from performing his ritual this year." Jane wove her arm through Amilie's and leaned close. "You know such a happy marriage is not normal."

"My mother and father were happy in their marriage."

"Mine seem happy most of the time, but my father never objects to mother's visits to friends and relatives. Lord and Lady Brompton never go anywhere without the other."

Amilie folded her hands together in her lap and bowed her head. "So when the Earl of Brompton goes to Town, Lady Brompton always accompanies him?"

"Always."

The two young ladies strolled arm-in-arm to the far side of the lake. Amilie had no need to speak after Jane began relating the story of the first ball of her come-out season.

Pausing to watch a pair of ducks waddle along the bank and slip into the water, the distant figure of a gentleman, coming their way from the direction of the Manor house, came into view.

He was cutting across the lawns. When he made his way around a copse of trees, Amilie knew at once who it was. Of the four gentlemen currently at Brompton Manor, George Mullerton was the only one short enough not to have to duck his head when passing under the lowest of the hanging tree branches.

Amilie heard a loud gasp beside her.

"I believe it is George coming in our direction. Is my bonnet straight? Are my ribbons tied neatly? Is my face clear of smudges?"

Amilie peered at Jane and nodded her head up and down.

Then George was upon them. Amilie did not recall seeing him advance anywhere so quickly before. Beads of sweat framed his upper lip. His breathing was ragged.

"Ladies," he said doffing his hat and gazing at Jane like a puppy eager to be petted.

Chapter Nineteen

Geoorge joined Amilie and Jane as they walked the path around the lake. Jane was not coy. Her entire being sparkled and her voice took on an added lilt as she shared news of mutual friends with George.

When they completed their circuit, George checked his timepiece and declared he was late for a meeting with his father and Lord Brompton. Then, after executing a clumsy bow, he dashed off toward the Manor house.

The two young ladies claimed the bench they had abandoned earlier. Jane's demeanor shifted from over-joyed to pensive. Amilie concentrated on the steady pattern of the ripples on the water to avoid intruding on Jane's thoughts.

With the features on Jane's face still for the first time since Amilie met her, Amilie could see she was not pretty, her eyes were too close together and a faded blue color, her nose tipped up at the end and her chin receded. But lush, golden hair provided the perfect frame for a face that took on a glowing beauty when animated.

"I want to apologize for dominating the conversation after Mr. Mullerton joined us. From now on, I need to damp my eagerness in his presence."

"Do not damp anything. Your joy brightens the day and lifts everyone's spirits."

"I hope I did not appear rattle-brained."

"I do not think George found you anything other than charming. He came a far distance at a speed I did not think him capable of, to join us for such a brief time. I believe because he was so eager to see you again."

A wide grin split Jane's face, rounding her cheeks and lighting up her eyes. "He was dripping wet from his hurry on this warm day. I longed to take my handkerchief and dab the moisture from his forehead."

"It is probably best you did not. I believe he meant to give an appearance of ambling along, minding his own business, when he happened to see us. Instead of the obvious hurried search he was making, cutting across lawns and stumbling down the hill to reach your side."

Jane Owens and Amilie Jasperton laughed until they each gasped for breath.

"He did appear in some hurry," Jane said. Her facial expression brightening.

"Join me when I ride tomorrow?" Amilie said.

"With delight. Brompton Manor has the loveliest of riding trails and the finest stables I have encountered in all of England."

"So far I have ridden along the path to the ice, house, over a wonderful trail that climbed gentle hills and meandered through woodlands and the short distance to explore the grotto."

"Which of the splendid horses are you riding?"

"Shining Star."

"Ah. She is a love. I rode her until the day Painted Wings came to the fence and nuzzled my hand. I fell in love with her at the very moment and have requested her ever since."

"Perhaps you might be persuaded to join my dance lessons too. George is a wonderful and patient partner, but it would be helpful for me to see the waltz performed by skilled partners."

Jane crossed her hands over her chest as her eyes widened into owl eyes. "Miss Jas . . . Amilie. You are kind to think me a skilled dancer. I will be happy to demonstrate the waltz for you tomorrow."

On the day of the picnic, Fitzhugh and George took turns rowing Amilie and Jane about the lake. This year the earl of Brompton had a footman row the boat containing himself and his beloved Lady Brompton to the middle of the lake. And this year he remained seated, but he sang lustily and managed to dramatize his effort with sweeping arm gestures. The crowd, who stood on the banks of the lake watching, cheered and clapped until the boat returned to the shore.

Each day Amilie and Jane spent hours together and grew as close as sisters. On the night of the assembly,

Amilie slipped into her new gown and twirled about in front of her cheval mirror.

"Perhaps after tonight, the prospect of going to London will not be so scary," she said to Helaine.

"Your dress is perfect, miss."

"I thank Miss Jane for invigorating me and giving me courage with her bubbly spirit and her helpful guidance."

"She can ease your way, miss."

That evening, three carriages, carrying the Brompton's and their guests, rolled past the gates of Brompton Manor. George and Fitzhugh had chosen to ride individual mounts. Jane and Amilie had a carriage of their own to give them enough space to keep their dresses from being crushed. Lord and Lady Brompton and Lady deVale occupied a second carriage. The Mullertons' and Mrs. Owens were being driven in the third.

The windows of the assembly room were ablaze. The carriages coming from Brompton Manor pulled in front and stopped. A group of villagers stood outside the assembly rooms and greeted the arrival of Lord and Lady Brompton, and the others in the party from Brompton Manor. After everyone alighted and entered the building, the invited villagers followed them into the large room where the assemblies were held.

Fitzhugh had not forgotten his promise to partner Amilie for her first set. He stood at her side waiting for the musicians to begin.

"You and Miss Owens get on well."

"She is just as I wished and has shared with me details of London's excitements and of her come-out."

"Are you planning a Season?"

"Perhaps not a come-out, but an introduction to London society on a smaller scale."

"London offers many entertainments. I am weary of them."

Amilie looked up at his profile. "But you plan to live there."

"I need to live somewhere, Miss Jasperton, and until I find another place, London it is." Fitzhugh's words filtered through his clenched teeth.

Amilie looked into his face and caught the pain that streaked his eyes. "My apology, Mr. Fitzhugh for speaking of painful things."

The musicians took seats, placed their music sheets on the stands and tuned their instruments. People began forming sets. Amilie tensed. Her gloved fingers clutched Fitzhugh's arm. He reached across and patted her hand then leaned down to whisper reassurance to her. "No one will be watching your feet, Miss Jasperton."

Amilie responded with a nervous laugh. "If I stumble and start to fall, I expect you to catch me before I find myself sprawled on the floor in a most unladylike fashion."

"A gentleman would do no less."

Amilie looked up at Fitzhugh and, despite an effort not to, giggled. The stiffness in her shoulders relaxed. "I have relied on your friendship to steady me in many ways. I will miss you."

Fitzhugh pursed his lips, glanced away, and steered her to the middle of a set.

Once she began to perform the steps to the dance, Amilie found the dance master had prepared her well. She partnered with a different gentleman for each of the following sets and did not once stumble or miss a step.

And then the waltz was announced.

Expecting George to keep his promise to partner her the first time she attempted a waltz in public, she looked around the room and spotted him, across the way, leading Jane Owens to the floor—his promise to partner her forgotten. She was delighted for Jane that George would partner her for the waltz, but all of the confidence she had gained as she finished each of the dances, collapsed into a ravine of doubt. She did not wish to perform her first public waltz with an untested partner.

Before she could take a chair and recover her senses, Fitzhugh's dark curls bobbed before her face as he dipped a deep bow, held out his arm and led her to the floor. She did not recall her feet touching the floor as the rhythm of the waltz caught her up; the musical notes wove a cocoon, locking her with Fitzhugh into a world where only the two of them existed. They spun around and around, his hands guiding her, his lips that had kissed her right in front of her eyes.

Then the music ended along with her fantasy. Amilie felt Fitzhugh's hands drop away and watched his lips tremble before he looked about the room and cleared his throat.

"Miss Jasperton, my compliments on your dancing skills. You prove yourself as adept at dance as you are at riding." And then he spun around on the balls of his feet and strode off toward the Assembly room's exit door.

Amilie remained standing where he left her until Jane took her arm and led her to a corner of the ballroom.

"You looked in such distress, standing there alone. I pray you are not upset over George standing with me for the waltz. He confided in me he felt it only proper to offer to aid you in your first public performance of the waltz, that he had promised you he would, but Fitzhugh threatened him."

Amilie stared at Jane. "Fitzhugh threatened George? Why on earth?"

"Given the look I saw in Mr. Fitzhugh's eye, he favors you, Amilie."

"He cannot."

"Well, whether he can or cannot, I believe he does."

Amilie took Jane's hand then bent her head close to Jane's ear. "We encountered one another in the hall one day. I lured him into kissing me. He thinks me wanton, I am sure. Then to make things worse, I wrote a note to him, confessing that I was hopelessly in love with him. He later told me I mistook my feelings of gratitude for his companionship during my time of suffering, for feelings of love."

"He kissed you?"

"Inadvertently."

"I never heard of someone kissing another person inadvertently."

"I behaved wantonly and caused him to lose control. He has not tried to kiss me again."

"Oh, I am so jealous. No gentleman, other than my father, has ever kissed me. What behavior did you exhibit that caused Mr. Fitzhugh to lose control?"

"I am not sure. I only remember pushing myself against him as his lips lowered to mine."

"Oh, how lucky for you. Do you long for George to kiss you, too?"

"I trust you will not breathe a word of this confidence. George is not under consideration by me for kissing."

Jane let out a huge sigh. "I have been so worried. I did not want to spoil our friendship, but I find George Mullerton irresistible."

"I believe you do, and we shall always be friends. I think George is fond of you."

"Do you? Do you think if I leaned against him, I could lure him into kissing me?"

Amilie and Jane laughed merrily. Amilie was relieved to have freed her friend from any constraint she might feel in her pursuit of George. And she would do all she could to facilitate their being together.

The chair in which the earl of Brompton had spent the evening was elevated above the floor of the dance floor giving him an unhindered view of interior of the assembly room. As the evening proceeded, he watched Fitzhugh with interest. When the waltz was announced, he saw Fitzhugh stop George and engage in a short but intense conversation. George had spun around and gone in the opposite direction. The next time the earl of Brompton saw George he was leading Miss Owens to the dance floor.

And then, the next thing he saw, Fitzhugh whirled into view with Amilie in his arms. Lord Brompton pondered the expression on Fitzhugh's face. It was not a benign expression, nor brotherly. It was a face filled with yearning.

When the music ended, the expression on Fitzhugh's face changed to the look of a hunted stag desperate to escape the hounds. He had spoken a few words to Amilie and exited the assembly room.

The earl of Brompton gestured a footman to his side and ordered him to find Lady Brompton and inform her he wished to speak with her at once. Then he instructed the footman to find pen, paper, and ink and bring them to him without delay.

He held a brief discussion with Lady Brompton, inked a short note, and sent the waiting footman off to deliver it.

With no carriage lanterns to light the way, Fitzhugh rode his horse along the dark road with care. At first light, he would leave Brompton Manor forever in spite of the earl of Brompton's demand he remain until the Mullertons' departed. He did not know if the terms of the trust fund the earl of Brompton had gifted him with could be rescinded, nor did he care. He could not watch George Mullerton strutting about in his lordly manner, examining things on the estate with a proprietary, lustful eye, including Amilie. He could not remain here, seeing her every day, and not suffer greatly. But, wherever he found himself he would have the memory of her in his arms as they performed a faultless waltz and the memory of her lips touching his to carry with him in his heart.

Fitzhugh finished a note to his assigned valet. His personal things were to be packed and sent to the Brompton's town house. He would retrieve them from there.

Perhaps a return to America would be wise.

His departure plans from Brompton Manor made, Fitzhugh toasted himself with a last snifter of Lord Brompton's fine brandy and tucked into bed. He forced his eyelids down as tight as he could to keep out unwanted visions. He allowed the sounds of the battle that had raged around him, the smells and feel of the heated, muggy air of New Orleans to fill his mind. These gruesome memories were sufficiently powerful to wipe out all other thoughts.

Fitzhugh did not hear the soft footfalls of his valet. "Sir?"

A candle was lighted, the flame danced before his eyes as he opened the lids wide enough to see who disturbed him.

"What do you want at this hour?"

"Sir, his lordship sent this note and insisted it be brought to you and read at once."

Fitzhugh sputtered but sat up and took the paper. "Hold the candle closer so I can see the words."

His eyes traveled down the paper. "Confound it. He commands me to an audience with him at the dower house before the cock crows."

"I believe his lordship means for you to present your-self at the dower house at once."

"Do not be impudent."

"Yes, sir. Will you require further assistance, sir?"

"When I return from the dower house, you are likely to find you have been returned to the duty of trimming candles."

Chapter Twenty

Fitzhugh shrugged into his jacket, pulled on his boots, ran his hands through his hair, and splashed his face with the tepid water remaining in his basin.

As he made his way to the dower house, the memory of seeing Amilie standing in the misty gloom of the grotto caused him to shiver.

The windows of the room the earl of Brompton used as a study glowed with faint light.

Fitzhugh waited for someone to respond to his tappings on the door. He grew more determined, as each second passed, to stand firm against any entreaty his guardian might make that he stay until the Mullertons departed.

The door cracked open. Fitzhugh pushed the door wider and strode past the earl of Brompton's valet without even a nod of his head. The door to the study was ajar. Pushing it open, Fitzhugh saw the earl of Brompton seated in a chair beside a roaring fire, reading.

"Ah, Fitzhugh, close the door and come have a seat. I hope I did not rouse you from sleep."

Fitzhugh moved into the room and said nothing as he settled into a chair across from the earl of Brompton. Leaning forward, he placed his elbows on his knees and laced his fingers together.

"You left the assembly in somewhat of a hurry. Was your stomach queasy again?"

"I am leaving for London. I will be off at dawn."

"But a week remains before the Mullertons' visit ends."

"So it does."

"What makes you so determined to leave before I give you permission?"

Fitzhugh rose to his feet and began to pace about the room as he spoke. "Your Lordship, I owe you everything and wish never to disappoint you. Your Lordship and Lady Brompton cared for me and provided me a wonderful life and an education at the finest schools. I am pleased you think highly enough of me to consider offering me the position of steward on your estates, but such a position would only cause me grief."

"Why would being my land steward cause you grief?"

"Because George is unbearable, and when your title passes to his father there can be no pleasure here for me."

"Is Amilie a part of your grief?"

Fitzhugh stopped pacing and gazed into the fire.

"Amilie will fill the position of the countess of Brompton with the grace and the dignity of the current countess of Brompton. She will always have my heart. I cannot stay."

"My beloved countess and I are releasing Amilie from all obligations to our wishes. She is free to choose her own future."

Fitzhugh made a strangled sound deep in his throat.

"Did she displease you in some way? Are you banishing her in the same way you banished her mother?"

Lord Brompton glowered at Fitzhugh. "I think that remark is out of place, Fitzhugh."

"My sincere regret for having made such a remark, Your Lordship."

"Amilie pleases us very much, Fitzhugh."

"Then why have you given her the freedom you refused her mother?"

"We are wiser now. The title will pass, time will pass, and one cannot order the future. I have come to accept this truth as I have grown older. I suppose when our daughter was young, I was caught up in my own importance."

Fitzhugh reached out and clutched the earl of Brompton's pale, cold hands in his own rosy, warm hands, then squatted down beside the earl of Brompton's chair. "I will leave Brompton Manor as planned and await further word from Miss Jasperton. Convey my offer to her. She can weigh her choices free of influence."

"She suits you well Fitzhugh. Perhaps one day you will row her to the middle of a lake and sing her a love song. My offer of the house and property that is not entailed is still available if you should wish it."

Fitzhugh hurried from the study and away from the dower house. Tears streamed down his face as entered the Manor house and climbed the stairs to his apartments for the last time.

The next morning Amilie felt at odds with everything around her. Something was amiss. She looked for Fitzhugh during the day, but made no inquiry about his absence until she returned to her apartments after dinner and an evening of cards.

"Helaine, is there any word below stairs about Mr. Fitzhugh? He has not taken ill, has he?"

"Gone to London, miss."

Amilie covered her face with her hands and moaned. He could not have gone without saying good-bye. "Are you sure they said gone and not going?"

"I am sure, miss."

"I believe I shall keep to my bed tomorrow, Helaine. If anyone inquires assure them I am fine but tired after the excitement of my first evening of dancing."

"Miss?"

"And send word to the stables I am canceling my lesson for the morning. Then explain to Lady Brompton there is no need for her to visit me."

"Of course, miss. Now into your nightclothes and I will fetch a tisane to aid your sleep. Did you enjoy the assembly, miss?"

"Very much. I was partnered for every dance. The strain of trying to remember the steps is likely the cause of my exhaustion."

"And Mr. George Mullerton partnered you for the waltz?"

"No, he waltzed with Miss Owens."

"But if you danced every dance, someone partnered you for the waltz."

"Mr. Fitzhugh was kind enough to rescue me from the sidelines."

"I see."

Helaine slipped the nightrail over Amilie's head and drew a shawl across her shoulders. "Sit by the fire, until I return with your tisane."

By the time Helaine returned to Amilie's apartments with the tisane, Lady Brompton was already there, wiping Amilie's tears and patting her hand.

"Leave the cup and you may go, Helaine," Lady Brompton said. "I will ring for you if there is further need."

Lady Brompton smoothed Amilie's hair, placed a finger under Amilie's chin, and lifted her head.

"What has caused you such upset, my child?"

Amilie gasped for sufficient breath to speak. "I cannot remain here any longer. I shall be gone by noon tomorrow."

"And go where?"

"The squire, in my home village, who took me in after my parent's accident and gave me a position as assistant governess, assured me I was welcome to return to his household at any time."

"Are you leaving because George is showing favoritism toward Jane?"

"I could not be happier for George and Jane."

"Because of Fitzhugh, then?"

Amilie looked down into her lap, her words came in a whisper. "I would have refused to marry George Mullerton even if you had insisted I must. I am hopelessly in love with Mr. Fitzhugh. And he is gone. I have driven him away from the home he loves."

"Rest tonight with an untroubled heart. Your grandfather will see you in the morning. He intended to have a private conversation with you today, but became caught up in the business of the estate. I think you will be pleased by what he will tell you."

Amilie looked at Lady Brompton. For the first time, she noticed a twinkle in her eyes. "I have the highest regard for you and Lord Brompton. You have been very kind to me, and I am grateful for the opportunity you gave me to visit my mother's home and to meet you. I will stay until I hear what Lord Brompton has to say. But, I do not plan to change my mind."

Lady Brompton rose and kissed Amilie's damp cheek. "Sleep well, dear child."

Chapter Twenty-one

The next morning Lady Brompton accompanied Amilie to the dower house. Lord Brompton, looking hale and hearty, was at his breakfast.

"Join me," the earl of Brompton said, sweeping his hand above the serving dishes. "Glad for the company."

"We have both had our breakfast, Brompton."

"Coffee then. All around," he said looking at the footman standing against the far wall.

The coffee poured and the serving dishes removed from the table, the earl of Brompton wiped toast crumbs from his lips, checked the front of his vest, and dabbed at a spot on his jacket.

"Lovely day," he said. "So much sunshine here. Shame we cannot take it with us when we go to London."

Amilie sat on the edge of her seat. Her shoulders

square to the table, her spine stiff as a riding crop. Her hands were in her lap, the fingers twined together.

Lord Brompton cleared his throat. "You look sprightly this morning, my dear granddaughter. Fitzhugh will be well pleased with your morning appearance. Some women of my acquaintance look rather dreary in the mornings."

"Brompton, that is quite unwarranted."

"Not you my dear. You look lovely at all times of day."

Amilie's eyelids fluttered up and down across her eyes. *What was he saying? It made no sense at all.*

"Brompton, do not tease Amilie with delay."

"Of course. Yes. The best thing." Lord Brompton grinned. "The news I have makes me so happy, I choke up and the words become difficult for me to say."

"Brompton."

"Cetainly," he said pushing himself to his feet and clearing his throat.

"My dear child, Fitzhugh has offered for you."

Amilie sprang up from her chair. "Fitzhugh? Surely, you mean George."

Lady Brompton moved to Amilie's side. "Fitzhugh requested permission to offer for you in the wee hours of the morning and Brompton has agreed. Now it is your decision to accept or refuse Fitzhugh's offer."

Lord Brompton wiped his cheeks. "The love and respect between the two of you was obvious, but the night of the assembly when you waltzed past me in Fitzhugh's arms, I knew I had no choice in the matter."

Amilie stood up. "He fled to London."

"To get away from the Mullertons, I fear. I never would admit the tension between Fitzhugh and George. Always thought, if not friends, they would come to understand they could be of use to one another. But I was wrong."

"I thank you for your kindness in my regard, your Lordship." Amilie sank down into her chair.

"I meant to speak to you earlier about this matter, Amilie. But Mullerton came to see me yesterday and a lengthy discussion ensued."

Amilie sipped from her lukewarm coffee. "I want nothing more than to be married to Mr. Fitzhugh. I will send him a note of my acceptance, but then how am I to proceed?"

Lady Brompton stood and gestured for Amilie to follow. "Come, we can discuss those things and enjoy the air while we stroll back to the Manor house."

Lady Brompton patted Lord Brompton's hand. "Rest now, Brompton. Tomorrow, if you are feeling strong, we will ride together. It has been a long time."

"A splendid idea, my love. This afternoon, I am planning to visit the stables to see my horses. I have missed them almost as much as I have missed you, my dear. Expect my return to the Manor house tomorrow. Have my apartments made ready."

Outside the dower house, Lady Brompton twined her arm around Amilie's. "The mantua-maker assures me she will have your new things finished before we leave for London. A special license will be obtained.

Fitzhugh will be settled by the time we arrive in Town. All of the arrangements for your wedding will be made from here."

"This is so sudden. My heart is swelled so, I can barely breathe."

"I should think you will adjust to the idea in a few days. Jane will listen to your joy and help you sort through any of your doubts or fears."

"I do like her a great deal."

"I am delighted the two of find enjoyment in one another. Perhaps one day the two of you can ease the relationship between Fitzhugh and George to the point they are at least civil to one another."

"Did you know Jane has had a *tendre* for George for a long time?"

"I will let Jane tell you; but, oddly enough, after Fitzhugh received Brompton's blessing to offer for you, Mr. Mullerton, in lieu of Jane's father not being here, requested an audience with Brompton the very next day. He proposed that George offer for Jane. And Brompton gave his blessing."

"I will write Fitzhugh at once. He will be happy to learn George and Jane will be wed."

"I have numerous things to see to." Lady Brompton squeezed Amilie's hand. "Shall I arrange for Jane to join you in a walk this afternoon?"

"Please. I am eager to speak with her."

Amilie and Jane sat together on a bench near the lake.

"I am to marry Mr. Fitzhugh, Jane."

Jane leaped to her feet, clapped her hands together then settled back down on the bench. Her face sobered as she looked at her new friend. "Do you wish to marry Mr. Fitzhugh? Or are you being forced to marry him because he kissed you?"

Amilie laughed. "Of course not. Not forced. I think I wanted to marry him from the first moment I saw him."

"Then I am delighted for you." Jane stood and twirled a little dance stopping to add her news. "Do you know Mr. Mullerton pleaded George's case before Lord Brompton after George indicated to his father a desire to offer for me? And when Lord Brompton gave his approval, Mr. Mullerton notified my mother he would be speaking with my father upon their return to town."

Amilie beamed her pleasure at Jane's news. "I am very happy for you, Jane."

"I was fearful you would be disappointed over losing the opportunity to marry George and would no longer wish to be my friend."

"By the time I became acquainted with George, my heart belonged to Mr. Fitzhugh. I wanted to respect my grandparents' wish for me and tried to have George find me suitable. It was hopeless. He was smitten with you."

"I could not hide my feelings for him and worried every moment you would think I coveted your rightful place."

"I have no sense of my rightful place in the world of the nobility. You will make a wonderful countess of Brompton, with no effort on your part. For me fulfilling that role would have been a struggle."

"But you would have been a wonderful countess of Brompton, Amilie."

"I would not have accepted an offer. My heart belongs to Fitzhugh, and it would not have been fair to George to marry him knowing he would never have my heart nor I his."

"When Mr. Fitzhugh and you were waltzing at the assembly it looked as though you were in a separate world."

"I believe we may have been unaware of anything around us until the music stopped. Now you must tell me, are you still waiting to experience George's kiss?"

Jane offered Amilie the smile of someone who is trying to keep a secret. "Oh, I must tell, George's lips are as soft as a baby's cheek."

Jane's eyes sparkled as she and Amilie began to laugh.

Amilie muted her laughter and cupped her hand to her ear.

"Do you hear the bird singing so beautifully, Jane? It is the song of a winter wren."

Chapter Twenty-two

By the night of the ball at Brompton Manor in honor of the Mullertons, Amilie had heard nothing from Fitzhugh. Her nerves were near the breaking point. Jane kept reassuring her that he was busy making arrangements for living space for the two of them and seeing to securing their future.

During the waking hours, the house was full of guests who had arrived ahead of time. There were several young people in residence. Amilie found most of them friendly. Jane had eased her introduction and, at her future mother-in-law's urging, kept up a lively social schedule for the younger set.

They rode during the day and played cards or performed at night. All complimented Amilie when it was her turn to play and sing. And with the number of young men present, there would be no lack of partners for the dances. But her smiles and laughter when she was in their company were forced. Her entire being longed for Fitzhugh. She was afraid to ask anyone if there was word from him in case bad news was being withheld from her until after the ball.

At night alone in her bed, doubts filled her thoughts. *Had his heart cooled? After he arrived in the lively atmosphere of London had he realized the last thing he wanted at this time in his life was a wife? Perhaps he had run off to India. Or had he come to the realization he had only wanted her because he thought George was going to marry her? And now that George did not want her, she had lost her appeal to him.*

Helaine made it impossible to forego going down for dinner before the ball. Dressed in the most elegant gown she had ever worn, with the diamond earrings, a gift from her grandparents, in her ears, she descended the stairs. Jane immediately came to her side. "You are breathtaking, Amilie. The gentleman around me gasped the moment they saw you at the top of the stairs."

Amilie blinked back her tears. "You are kind to say so, Jane. I shall try to put Fitzhugh out of my mind and enjoy this festive evening."

The long dinner was over. Guests who lived close enough to travel from home for the ball itself and the supper after were arriving. Lord and Lady Brompton and the Mullertons were busy greeting the guests. Amilie and Jane stood to one side of the ballroom, watching the activity around them.

"One day Jane, you will be the hostess of these affairs. You have demonstrated your ability by organizing the activities for the younger set during the past few days. I am delighted for you."

"And you must be a frequent guest when that time comes."

Moments later, they saw Lady Brompton speak to the assembled musicians, a country dance was called, and people took to the dance floor. Amilie was partnered by a gangly young man who attacked the dance with fervor. By mid-evening she was tired, declined the opportunity for another dance, and went to sit near a group of older women.

She fanned herself and watched the dancers. Several of the older women near her gasped and pointed in the direction of the ballroom doors. Amilie turned. A gentleman in riding clothes, a large tear evident on the sleeve of his coat, a smear of dirt across his forehead stood in the doorway. Amilie found herself on her feet moving toward the door with long strides. Fitzhugh caught up to her in seconds. "What happened to you?" Amilie asked.

"A small accident with my horse. He is fine. I am fine."

Everything turned hazy. Time turned endless. The lighted ballroom turned into shadows on the terrace.

And in the magic of those shadows, Fitzhugh drew

her to him and touched his lips to hers. Her heart raced for a very long time before he pulled back and gazed into her upturned face.

"I love you dearly, Amilie."